cl

Th   man Dies

af

THE OLD MAN DIES

THE OLD MAN DIES

by GEORGES SIMENON

TRANSLATED FROM THE
FRENCH BY *Bernard Frechtman*

A HELEN AND KURT WOLFF BOOK
HARCOURT, BRACE & WORLD, INC.   *New York*

M

c · l

THE OLD MAN DIES

I

From the cashier's desk where she was sitting and smiling vaguely, Fernande saw the couple enter and realized at once that they were newcomers. They were both very young and were wearing new clothes from head to foot, like newlyweds, which they no doubt were. As soon as they crossed the threshold, they tried to conceal their surprise and hesitation.

Antoine had also spotted them from the back room but had not bothered, and it was François, the redheaded waiter, who had gone to welcome them.

"This way, please . . ."

He gave them a bad table, in the middle of the restaurant, and the young people glanced at a corner table without daring to say anything. In any case, if they had asked for it, François would have said that it was reserved.

The buxom Liselotte went to take their coats and, as she passed the cashier's desk, winked at the boss's wife.

The Ambassador and his guests had not yet arrived, but their table for eight was set in the back room, which the staff called "the Senate" because it was reserved for good customers and prominent persons.

The couple, who were from the provinces, had probably been living in Paris only a short time. While strolling about the Central Market, they had noticed a restaurant that looked more or less like the others, though a bit more attractive because of the hams and salamis that hung in the window.

The signboard was also modest, and the young people were taken a little aback when François handed them a menu on elegant paper and as big as a folio.

Yet the tables in the front room were old marble-topped cast-iron tables, the bar was a standard tin bar, and in a black frame on the faded green wall above it was the "Law regarding Drunkenness in Public."

"I suggest that you start with beef broth or *cochonnades*."

From her post between the two rooms and facing the cloakroom, Fernande was in the habit of taking everything in. She saw her husband, who was wearing a dark blue suit, bend forward over two newspapermen who were accompanied by young women whose pictures had been in the papers and magazines.

Behind the glass partition she could also see the chef bustling about his electric stoves.

The British Embassy had rung up to reserve a table for eight, which had created a certain nervousness in the establishment. Antoine had sent out for flowers. Although he had shaved at eleven in the morning, he had gone upstairs a little before seven to run his electric razor over his cheeks a second time.

Almost all the tables were occupied. The two youngsters had decided on the *cochonnades* and were astounded to see so many different kinds of pork delicacies on the trolley that was rolled up to their table. The block of country butter that sat enthroned in the middle amazed the woman in particular.

Where was Auguste at the time? No doubt, as usual, at one of the tables of what was called "the bistrot." The restaurant was his. He had bought it in 1913 with his savings and a little money that his brother had loaned him. He had never dreamed that he would be sent to the front the following year.

At that time, what was now the Senate was occupied by the kitchen, and the present kitchen, which was spick and span behind its glass partition, was the bedroom.

Two Rolls-Royces stopped at the curb. Antoine hurried to the door. The Ambassador and his guests were not wearing evening clothes and walked to their table unostentatiously, though everybody watched them.

It was not the first time that important persons had come to dine. The guest of honor, at the Ambassador's right, was a middle-aged woman who must have had her face lifted, for her features were completely immobile. She gazed idly and as if condescendingly at the curiosities the diplomat pointed out to her.

Fernande recognized him. He had lunched there two or three times without saying who he was. He brought to his guest's attention, with the pride of someone who had discovered an extraordinary place, the glass partition that made it possible for diners to follow the preparing of the dishes. Then he pointed to the paintings on the walls, among which were three Utrillos.

Old Auguste had got them for almost nothing. A friend from Riom, with whom he had gone to school, ran a restaurant at the time in Montmartre, at the very top of Rue du Mont-Cenis. Auguste had loaned him some money and, as his old schoolmate was unable to repay it, had accepted the pictures in return.

Antoine was taking the order and discreetly advising his guests. To begin with, galantine of suckling pig, a few slices

5

of Auvergne sausage, and a Saint-Flour dainty. Then, leg of lamb accompanied by a red Chanturgue wine that had a slight taste of violets.

Everything was going well. Everything was running smoothly. It was half past nine, and two tables had already asked for the check.

Auguste had taken down from the wall a faded photograph of the restaurant as it had been in 1920, with himself at the bar, in shirt sleeves, and his wife a bit off to the side. He was showing it to two out-of-town customers who had dined too well and whom he had just given a glass of brandy on the house.

Of course, he had poured a drink for himself too, after a furtive glance in the direction of the cashier's desk and of his son, for he was not supposed to drink. He always took advantage of a busy moment to sit down at a table and help himself to a glass of wine or spirits. Whenever his eye caught his daughter-in-law, he would smile at her with a look of complicity.

Antoine was strict. Fernande was not. Why deprive a man close to eighty of his last little pleasures?

As always, there was the hum of conversation in both rooms and the clink of glasses and clatter of plates. One no longer noticed the noise, just as one no longer noticed the smell of cooking and of wine.

Outside, vegetables were being piled up all over the Market, and the sheds were already lit up.

Fernande's eyes followed her husband, the waiters, and the customers who were putting on their coats and moving toward the door. Nobody on the staff slept enough, and toward the middle of the evening everyone began to feel pleasantly drowsy.

The two provincials had left, and Auguste was now standing near the newlyweds, to whom he was showing the photograph.

She could not hear what he was saying. Always the same
story. How he had left Riom for Paris at the age of fifteen;
how in those days throats were slit in the dark streets around
the Market; how he sent for specialties from Auvergne, his
birthplace, including the big loaves of grayish bread that
were in the window.

She had to take her eyes off him for a few seconds. Her
husband had nodded to her on his way to the kitchen to let
her know that everything was all right and that the English
party was pleased.

When she looked around again, Auguste was swaying. He
was holding on to a chair, which was toppling under the pres-
sure. Clinging to the red and white checked tablecloth, he
dragged with him the plates and food of the young couple.

There was a crash, but no actual confusion. François, the
redheaded waiter, was the first to get to the old man and was
about to grab his shoulders when Antoine pushed him aside
and lifted up his father, whom François took by the feet.

It had happened so quickly that one would have thought
the scene had been rehearsed. Joseph, who had been working in the restaurant for thirty years, was already picking up
the dishes and apologizing. The young people, upset and bewildered, were staring at the old man who was being helped
to a door near the desk that opened on the hallway of the
building. Fernande had had time enough to see that her
father-in-law's face was purple, that one of his eyes was shut,
and that the other had a fixed look.

She did not leave her post, from where she heard footsteps
in the narrow, ill-lit stairway.

Antoine and François were puffing when they got to the first floor, where they entered the low-ceilinged apartment of the two old people.

Eugénie had been put to bed at eight o'clock, as every evening. She was seventy-nine years old, a year older than her husband, and was no longer in her right mind.

During the day, she was put into a chair near the window. The servant, Madame Ledru, fed her as one does a child.

Being half asleep, she did not realize what was going on. Perhaps she was merely surprised to see the lamps lit.

"Go get Madame Ledru," ordered Antoine.

The servant occupied a small room facing the court. She arrived in a purple bathrobe.

"Help me undress him and put him to bed . . . François, you can go down now . . . Tell my wife I'll be right back."

He could not leave the restaurant in the lurch. Downstairs, the rhythm must not be broken or changed.

Auguste was still breathing, but with a wheeze that distorted his mouth, as if he had no control of the movement of his lips. What was most impressive was his open eye that looked off into space.

"Phone Dr. Patin . . . Tell him it's urgent . . . Call me as soon as he comes."

Antoine walked away reluctantly from the bed where his mother and father were lying side by side. At the threshold, he hesitated. What could he do? He hadn't the slightest notion. The doctor, who lived two blocks away, on Rue Pierre-Lescot, would be there in a few minutes. Downstairs, it was a little like going on stage from the wings. Antoine went through the dark hallway of the old building and, by pushing the door near Fernande's cash desk, returned to the light and warmth of the restaurant. He saw the flowers on the Ambassador's table, and the kitchen, where things were in full swing.

The newlyweds, who had not left, had lost their appetite and were pale. They were eating a dish of veal tripe that had just been served. Other customers watched Antoine as he walked to the desk.

"He's breathing," he whispered to his wife, whose only reaction was to flutter her eyelids.

Some tiny bits of glass on the floor indicated where old Auguste had fallen. On one of the greenish walls a brighter rectangle showed where the photograph of the father and mother in 1920 belonged. Joseph had picked it up and, since the frame was broken, had handed it, as if it were a relic, to Fernande, who had slipped it under the cashbox.

The dishes kept coming from the kitchen. The diners were now up to the cheese and dessert. The smell of cigar smoke began to mingle with that of cooking.

Antoine continued to keep an eye on everything, particularly in the Senate. He played the role of both proprietor and headwaiter, but because of the style of the establishment he wore a dark blue suit instead of the customary evening clothes.

"My father had a dizzy spell," he said to the Ambassador.

The woman in the party was looking at him with limpid, impassive eyes. Who was she? The others treated her with marked respect. Wasn't she more or less related to the royal family?

A minor king from the Near East had once come for dinner with a vivacious party and two bodyguards. He had been hard to please because he did not eat pork, which was the restaurant's specialty.

Had Patin arrived? He had been the family doctor for al-

9

most forty years. He had treated Antoine and his two brothers when all three children had come down with scarlet fever at the same time. The family did not yet have the apartment on the first floor, and the children slept in cots on the top floor, in a maid's room with a sloping ceiling and window.

His wife's eyes seemed to be asking him a question. He looked around to be sure that things were going right, then disappeared again and went up the stairs three at a time.

As soon as one left the warm odors of cooking, one entered a domain that smelled of poverty, for most of the tenants were people who lived from hand to mouth.

Madame Ledru had put out the ceiling light and left on only a bedside lamp. She was sitting by the head of the bed and holding the old man's wrist while looking at her watch.

His breathing seemed weaker. From time to time, Auguste would make two or three convulsive movements, as if his whole body were protesting against what was happening to it.

"How many?"

"His pulse keeps changing all the time . . . Just a moment ago it was a hundred forty . . . and now I hardly feel it."

"What about the doctor?"

"He's out seeing a patient . . . An accident in a butcher shop . . . His wife's trying to reach him . . . She gave me the name of another doctor who lives on Rue Étienne-Marcel. I called up. He promised to come right away."

The mother was sleeping, unconscious of what was going on around her.

Antoine went downstairs again. It was his duty to be there —at least for the big table—when brandy was served. As for Fernande, she could not go up because it was the time when more and more customers asked for the check.

Antoine managed to smile. He had adopted that smile years before, and he automatically hurried over as soon as anyone raised his hand a few inches.

The English party seemed satisfied, except the princess or duchess, who was still frozen and impenetrable. She refused the marc brandy but accepted the old Armagnac in a large liqueur glass. Three minutes later the glass was empty.

A car stopped. Antoine waited a few minutes. When he went upstairs, he found a man whom he did not know, a man of uncertain age and with thinning hair.

It was the doctor from Rue Étienne-Marcel. No sooner did he open his mouth than old Dr. Patin arrived panting and puffing. The two men shook hands and exchanged a questioning look.

There was no need for them to use a stethoscope on the patient. Auguste's face was growing more and more purple, and when one of the doctors passed his hand in front of the one open eye, the pupil did not react.

"No point in taking him to the hospital," muttered Patin as he shook hands with Antoine.

"Can anything be done?"

"The end may come at any moment . . . On the other hand, he may hold out for hours . . ."

The doctors withdrew to a corner of the room and conversed in a low tone, while Antoine, who felt hesitant and useless, remained standing near the bed.

He was about to go down again. He could hardly bear the sight of that eye which looked nowhere, of that twisted mouth. He did not recognize his father. It was not a man who was lying on the bed but an unconscious thing that would soon be stark and stiff.

Just as he was about to step back, he thought he caught a kind of slight gleam in the staring eye. It resembled a look of surprise, and at the same moment the sound of breathing stopped.

"Doctor!" he called.

Patin rushed over, touched the eyelids, leaned forward, and pressed his cheek against Auguste's chest.

When he straightened up, he murmured, "It's over, Antoine . . . Have you been in touch with your brothers?"

"Not yet."

"How's the judge getting along?"

"He's all right. He's the one who's handling the Mauvis affair."

"And Bernard?"

Antoine's face clouded over.

"I haven't heard from him for months."

Patin understood. He had known them as little children and as teen-agers. He had attended the marriages of Antoine and of Ferdinand. He knew the family history by heart.

"Convey my condolences to your wife."

The two doctors left together by the steep, narrow stairway.

"Can I call in old Marinette to lay him out?" asked Madame Ledru.

He nodded, went downstairs, opened the small door, and, as he went by, whispered to his wife, "It's over."

He got caught up in his work again, in the evening routine, until the last customer would have left and the iron shutters would be closed.

To Joseph too, who was sixty-eight and walked with his

toes turned out, then to François, then to Jules, who stood behind the bar and was in charge of the wines, Antoine repeated, in a more and more natural voice, "It's over."

Then to Julien Bernu, the chef, "It's over."

Liselotte, who was very buxom and appetizing in her black silk uniform, had no need to make an effort to smile at the customers when she helped them on with their coats. She was too young, too full of vitality.

The last customers had left shortly after eleven, and Antoine was now waiting to close the shutters. His father always waited with him to shut up shop, and for the two of them it was a kind of rite.

When Fernande had finished her accounts, she left by the small door and went up to the second floor, where the couple had an apartment directly above that of the old people. She took with her the green metal box that contained the receipts.

Jules, who got dressed more quickly than the others, went off with his hands in his pockets and his coat collar turned up, for it was a cold March evening.

Behind the bar was a trap door that opened on to a stairway leading to the cellar, and Antoine went, as he did every night, to insert the iron bar that closed it and to put on the padlock.

The two women dishwashers left by the door of the building. The staff hardly knew them, for such help never stayed long. At times one of the waiters had to hunt for men in the street to do the dishes.

Julien Bernu, the chef, was wearing an elegant camel's-hair coat, and a sports car was waiting for him at the corner.

"See you tomorrow, boss."

He hesitated, wondering whether he ought to add something, and finally shook Antoine's hand with a firmer grip than usual.

The rest of the staff did the same. They trickled out one after the other and went on with their personal lives.

Only two lights were left on. There was smoke around them, rather like a fog, and the smell of food had ceased to be appetizing.

The shutters were closed from the outside by means of a crank that was kept behind the bar. The Market was in full swing, and trucks were invading all the neighboring streets.

Fifty years before, and even after the First World War, the bar stayed open until dawn. It was frequented in those days by all kinds of people, including tramps and streetwalkers who dozed with their backs against the wall.

Antoine went outside. The night before, his father had followed him. They had both been silent. They had heard the rattle of the big shutter as it descended jerkily and then the noise of the narrower one that protected the door.

He had to go back by way of the corridor and then put away the crank. Antoine remained standing behind the bar for a moment, looking at the bottles on the shelves. He finally chose a marc brandy and poured himself a glass, which was unusual, for all he ever drank was a bit of wine with his meals.

Then he put out the lights, walked to the corridor, and closed the small door. He had checked to see that everything was in order in the kitchen and at the sink. He trudged up the stairs with his shoulders bowed. When he entered his parents' bedroom, he was surprised to find an old woman whom he did not know.

"I've done the best I could, sir. I thought you'd be pleased if I brought four candles and some holy water. You can give me whatever you like . . ."

It was the old maid whom he had heard about, the one who looked after all the dead bodies in the neighborhood. She had a round, gaping face with big blue innocent eyes, and she wore black clothes that must have dated from twenty years before.

He opened his wallet and handed her a few bills, while she pointed to his mother, who was still sleeping in the wooden bed.

"How is she?"

"She didn't bat an eyelash when we took the body away."

Antoine did not know where they had put his father. He crossed the old-fashioned living room where he had done his homework when he was a child and had played with his two brothers. The kitchen had served as a storeroom, since the family ate in the restaurant before the customers came.

Auguste's body was stretched out on Madame Ledru's bed, in the servant's bedroom. A towel was wrapped around the head to keep the jaw from dropping. Both eyes were closed, and the face had lost the weird look it had had earlier.

The hands were clasped over a rosary that did not belong to anyone in the family.

Fernande stood and watched her husband, waiting to see his reactions. As he remained motionless and silent, she murmured, "It seems that it's Marinette who . . ."

Two of the candles were lit, and a sprig of holly was lying in a finger bowl that probably contained holy water.

Antoine did not pray. They had not been taught to pray.

He felt very tired, and he remembered that he still had to inform his brothers.

Madame Ledru made a suggestion: "It would be better if I sat up with him, because I don't mind not sleeping . . . If necessary, I can lie down for a while on the couch in the living room."

Everything suddenly looked so old, so decrepit! Auguste had always been against any change whatever in the apartment where his wife herself had become a kind of object that was moved about from time to time in the course of the day.

"Come along . . ."

They went up to the second floor. The apartment was laid out in the same way, but the colors were brighter, the furniture was modern, and there was light.

He took off his jacket while his wife unhooked her black dress and then shook her brown hair.

"Are you going to call Ferdinand first?"

He nodded, picked up the telephone, and dialed the number. While waiting for an answer, he loosened his tie a little.

At Sceaux Park, where Ferdinand lived with his wife and son in a modern apartment house, the bell seemed to be ringing in empty space.

"Maybe you dialed the wrong number."

He kept listening. He seemed bored rather than sad.

"Hello . . . Is that you, Véronique?"

His sister-in-law spoke in a hushed voice.

"Is Ferdinand in?"

"He's sleeping, poor thing . . . I had to give him a sleeping pill because the Mauvis affair is getting him down . . . What's the matter, Antoine? . . . Why are you calling so late? . . . Has anything happened to your mother?"

"To my father . . ."

"Is he sick?"

"He died."

"Of what?"

"The doctor didn't tell me . . . I didn't even think of asking . . . I suppose it was a stroke . . . He was all blue . . ."

"Is he at the hospital?"

"No. At home, in the maid's room."

"Do you think I should wake Ferdinand? Is there anything he can do?"

"I think he'll be angry if we don't inform him."

"I don't know . . . You may be right . . . Hold the wire."

More than two minutes went by, during which time there were several clicks. At one point, a choked voice kept repeating, "Arthur . . . Arthur . . . Are you still there? . . . Do you hear me?"

It was a woman's voice and sounded far away. A moment later it gave way to Ferdinand's.

"Hello . . . That you, Antoine?"

"Yes . . . Excuse me for waking you . . ."

"You did the right thing . . . My wife's been plying me with medicines . . . I've been running a temperature the last three days with a sore throat, but the investigation has reached such a point that I can't stay home . . . The reporters are after me from morning to night. I half expect them to camp on my doorstep . . . So Papa's dead? . . . What time did it happen?"

"I didn't notice . . . around ten o'clock . . ."

"What time is it now?"

"Ten past twelve."

"Why didn't you call me earlier?"

"The restaurant was jammed, and there was a party of eight with the British Ambassador."

"A stroke?"

"Patin didn't tell me."

He repeated, "He was all purple."

"Did he know he was dying?"

"I don't think so."

"Where did it happen?"

"He was chatting with some customers, in the restaurant . . . Suddenly he fell down, dragging the tablecloth and everything on the table . . ."

"Did he say anything?"

"Nothing."

"Have you called Bernard?"

"Not yet."

"Have you seen him recently?"

"No. Have you?"

"I caught sight of him in a taxi about a month ago. Luckily, he didn't see me . . . I think I'd better drop by . . . What do you think?"

"There's nothing more one can do."

"I know. But if Bernard comes, there'll surely be a discussion, and it would be better if I were there."

"As you like."

Fernande asked him, "Is he coming?"

Her husband nodded and then looked up Bernard's number in an address book. When last heard from, he was living on Boulevard Rochechouart. Things were no doubt going to start getting complicated.

The telephone rang in an apartment that Antoine had

never seen, and a man's voice, which was unfamiliar, answered: "Who's speaking?"

Antoine could hear the sound of music and voices and the clinking of glasses.

"I think I've got the wrong number."

"Whom do you want to talk to?"

"To Bernard Mature."

"Bernard, eh! . . . Good old Bernard . . . Well, old boy, Bernard's not here."

The man was drunk, and someone was taking the phone from him. This time it was a woman's voice at the other end.

"Hello. This is Nicole."

"It's me, Nicole."

"Antoine? What's happened? Why are you phoning at this hour?"

"Isn't Bernard there?"

Even if she had been drinking, she had her wits about her.

"He's away for the moment," she answered cautiously, as if on the defensive.

"Out of town?"

"Why do you ask?"

"Because I have a piece of bad news for him."

"What is it?"

"Father died."

He was the only one who treated her like a sister-in-law, though she had been living with his brother for five years. They had both thought there was no point in marrying.

"That's too bad," she murmured, then added, in another tone, "Be quiet, all of you! There's been a death in the family." She continued, "Excuse me . . . Some friends of Bernard dropped in. They thought he was here and brought a few bottles. I don't know how to get rid of them. They think they're at home . . . Listen, Antoine, I'm really upset . . . Today's Friday, isn't it? . . . That's right, Saturday, since it's past midnight . . . Bernard drove south on Thursday with a friend. They may be in on a big real-estate deal."

Bernard was always expecting to be in on big deals, whether real-estate or not, on the Riviera or elsewhere.

"I know they had an appointment tonight at the Carlton Bar, but I don't know where they're staying."

"When is he due back?"

"He didn't say. It depends on the deal. But, all the same, he has to be informed, doesn't he? How did it happen?"

"He suddenly collapsed in the restaurant."

"A heart attack?"

"I don't know . . . A half hour later, he was dead."

"Is Ferdinand with you?"

"I'm expecting him."

"I'll do my best to find him . . . If I phone all the hotels I may get the right one."

Fernande questioned him again: "Where is he?"

"In Cannes, so she says. It's not necessarily true. There are several people at Nicole's place drinking and playing music."

"You think she'll come?"

"Her? What for?"

"I don't know . . . Are you getting undressed?"

"Not before I see Ferdinand."

"Véronique'll come with him."

It was inevitable, for Ferdinand was so nearsighted that he had never driven a car, and now that he had one his wife acted as chauffeur. She drove him to the courthouse every morning and picked him up in the evening. At noon he lunched frugally at the snack bar in the courthouse or in a little restaurant nearby.

"What do you think's going to happen?"

"I have no idea. It'll depend on Bernard."

"And Véronique."

"You think Véronique will make difficulties?"

"Perhaps more than Bernard . . . How about some coffee."

"Not a bad idea."

He smoked little, for he could not allow himself to smoke in the restaurant. He contented himself with an occasional cigarette, which he seldom had time to finish.

In five hours he would be up and about, to do his marketing, as he did every morning. Of course, he did not have far to go.

It was Jules who ran the bar in the morning and served the local customers.

At noon Antoine would put on his blue suit, and the two rooms would gradually fill up. By three o'clock they would be empty again. That enabled him to sleep a little, until about half past six, at which time he took a shower and dressed again.

Someone knocked at the door of the apartment below. The floors were so worm-eaten that one could hear what went on all through the house. Madame Ledru must have answered that Antoine and his wife were upstairs. Fernande went to open the door just as Ferdinand and Véronique reached the landing.

The two brothers did not kiss. They had never in their life kissed each other. They shook hands and looked at each other with a grave expression. Véronique, however, kissed both Antoine and Fernande.

"What a misfortune . . ."

And her husband retorted with his usual common sense, "At his age it was to be expected. The important thing is that he didn't suffer . . . What's surprising is that Mama wasn't the first to go . . . As a matter of fact, how is she?"

"She wasn't aware of anything. She was sleeping."

"Do you think she still recognizes what goes on around her?"

"It's hard to say . . . At times one has the impression that she comes to herself, that she's trying to say something . . . When that happens you'd swear she was fighting against a kind of fog, but it doesn't last and she falls back into her state of torpor."

"It seems that Father's been put into the maid's room."

"That was done so as not to move Mama . . . I suppose that tomorrow we'll have to set up a mortuary chapel in the living room . . . There'll be quite a crowd. All his friends from Riom and the Auvergnats in Paris."

For Auguste had been president of the Association of Auvergnats in Paris.

Ferdinand was fifty-three. He wore thick glasses and was almost completely bald. Véronique, though she had become stout, did not look her age.

"Won't that be troublesome?"

"I hesitate to close the restaurant until the funeral. That's not how things are done in the business. Usually one closes only on the day of the funeral."

"By the way, has the priest come?"

"No. I didn't think of sending for him."

"Father was a choirboy when he was a child. Of course, he stopped going to church, but all the same it would be a good thing if you informed the parish. People wouldn't understand your not letting the church know."

Fernande came in with coffee and cups. The armchairs and couch were covered with blue leather, and a red wall-to-wall carpet concealed the defects in the flooring.

"Someone rang the bell downstairs."

"Who could it be?"

They all stood still and listened. Madame Ledru opened the door, spoke in a low voice, and then shut the door.

Light footsteps were heard on the stairs.

"I bet it's Nicole," said Fernande as she stood up.

And when she opened the door, it was indeed Nicole whom they saw in the doorway.

She looked at them, one after the other, as if her visit were the most natural thing in the world, and took off her leopard-skin coat as she walked in.

"I thought it would be better if I came."

Fernande, who was in her bathrobe, went off to get another cup.

"Where is he?"

"On the first floor, in Madame Ledru's room."

"Why isn't he in his bed?"

"Because my mother was already in it," replied Antoine irritably.

II

There was an embarrassing silence. No one knew where to look. Ferdinand was only three years older than Antoine, but one would have thought that the difference in age, instead of ceasing to matter, had increased as time went by. Perhaps it was because of Ferdinand's profession. To the family he was the judge, someone important, a person who knew things of which the others were completely ignorant.

There had been a period, during their adolescence, when the two brothers were real friends. In those days Ferdinand took Antoine more or less under his wing. Neither of them bothered about Bernard, whom they regarded as a child.

Each had lived his life in his own way. Each of them had married. Ferdinand had lived in La Rochelle at first. Then he had been assigned to Poitiers, where he had remained for eight years before getting a post in Paris. He had aged more rapidly than the others, so much so that it was hard to imagine that he had ever been young.

One felt that he took life seriously, that he gave every problem the same scrupulous attention, whether it had to do with his professional duties, his family, or himself.

Antoine, who was a head taller than he and whose brown hair was not even thinning, seemed to be of another breed.

What were the two brothers thinking about as Nicole observed first one and then the other? Had they not been expecting this confrontation for a long time? Nevertheless, it had taken them unawares, in the middle of the night, with Ferdinand fighting against a sore throat and Antoine hardly able to keep his eyes open.

"Tell me, Ferdinand . . ."

Nicole's tone was always slightly formal when she spoke to the judge or his wife, whereas she felt completely at ease with Antoine. She was only twenty-eight and was pretty, chic, and vivacious. She came from another world.

Ferdinand looked at her with his nearsighted eyes, and she continued without the slightest embarrassment, "I know that it's none of my business, but, since Bernard is out of town, I'm obliged to speak for him . . . You who know about such things, don't you think that seals should have been affixed?"

"To what?"

"I don't know . . . to the dead man's apartment . . . to the safe . . ."

"What safe?"

Antoine felt more ill at ease than his brother, for he knew that the question had been directed at him, and he suspected that Ferdinand would not completely side with him.

"I don't think," said the examining magistrate, "that my father ever had a safe. . . Is that right, Antoine?"

"There's none in the house."

Nicole was nevertheless determined.

"All the same, he must have put his will somewhere."

There was an almost oppressive silence. Fernande brought a cup, filled it with coffee, then looked for a place to sit down. She had heard everything from the kitchen. Everyone was looking at Antoine.

"Father never mentioned a will to me."

"Didn't he have a notary?"

"It wasn't like him to put his affairs into the hands of a notary."

"He had a bank account, didn't he?"

"If he did, he didn't tell anyone."

Old Auguste was born in Saint-Hippolyte, a village near Riom with a population of three hundred. His father, who was a day laborer, could neither read nor write.

At the age of twelve, Auguste was already working in a fruit store, near the Law Court, and slept in the back room with his clothes on. At fifteen, he took a train and went to Paris alone.

"Ferdinand ought to know better than I what's to be done in such a case."

Ferdinand was embarrassed and looked at his wife as if to ask her for advice.

"It depends . . . There was once a written agreement between Father and Antoine."

It had been drawn up after the war, in 1945. Antoine had come back from Germany, where he had been a prisoner for more than four years. He hesitated about going back to his job of cook at the Strasbourg Tavern, where he had been working in 1939.

He was twenty-seven years old and unmarried. At the time, there was only a small restaurant on the ground floor. In the window were hams and sausages and big loaves of dark bread from Auvergne that were delivered three times a week.

Their mother did the cooking, and there was only one waiter.

Auguste was not yet an old man. During the war he had made a lot of money, thanks to the food he managed to bring in from Auvergne.

A new clientele had begun to frequent the restaurant. Newspapermen and theater people had discovered what they called Mother Mature's cooking.

"Son, why not stay with me instead of going off and working for someone else? We could set up another room, a bigger kitchen . . ."

Ferdinand, who was still in La Rochelle, already had a child. Bernard, who had not finished school, worked vaguely in the film industry and came to see their father only when he needed money.

Antoine finally let himself be talked into joining his father, and as the plan for enlarging the establishment grew more and more definite, he became enthusiastic. It was he who had had the idea of a glass-enclosed kitchen that made it possible for the customers to see the food being prepared.

For twenty-five years his mother had been satisfied with cooking four or five dishes, each on a given day.

She, too, was from Saint-Hippolyte, where her father had a small farm. She had gone to school with Auguste, who ran into her again when he went back to see his brother. She was twenty at the time.

Thereafter, their history was that of most of the shopkeepers in the neighborhood. After stinting for years, they were able to buy a business that it took them a long time to finish paying for. Then, long years without a day's rest and without the idea of a vacation ever occurring to them.

They were both on the floor below, Auguste with two candles burning at his side, and his wife, who had been unconscious for about a year of what went on around her.

They had once been young. At night, before going to sleep in the wooden bed which they had bought secondhand two days before their marriage, they would reckon up the day's receipts together, delighting in the money that came in and in being able to pay off their debts, one after the other.

"When we no longer owe anything . . ."

For a long time that was their sole aim. Then there had been Ferdinand, who crawled about on all fours in the sawdust of the restaurant and on the tiles in the kitchen.

They knew little of Paris other than the neighborhood of the Central Market and the few streets in the vicinity.

Auguste had a big bluish-black mustache. Standing behind his bar with his sleeves rolled up, he was proud of his bulging muscles.

Then Antoine was born. The two children slept in their parents' bedroom, and Antoine remembered certain evenings when his mother peeled vegetables in the kitchen while his father arranged his bottles.

Between Ferdinand and Bernard there was a difference in age of six years. The bedroom was no longer big enough for all of them, and, since there was no other solution, they rented a garret on the sixth floor for the two older boys.

At first, the youngsters were frightened. They were afraid of being alone at the top of the house, which seemed to them enormous and which swarmed with people they did not know.

They slept in the same bed so as to comfort each other. In winter it was very cold, and they wore long cotton-flannel nightshirts.

Ferdinand was sent to school. Then it was Antoine's turn. They played in the street with other children.

In those days it seemed to Antoine and Ferdinand that they would never separate.

They were now looking at each other sheepishly. Although

the father's body was still warm, a stranger had just put her finger on the sore spot.

"Has anyone looked in the drawers?" she asked.

Both brothers were shocked, but they knew the question was valid, and they realized what it implied.

"No one has looked for anything in the apartment," said Antoine, who felt that the question had been aimed at him.

"When Father collapsed, I carried him up to the first floor, and I had to go down while Madame Ledru phoned the doctor. I couldn't stay away from the restaurant, which was full . . ."

It was impossible to read anything into Ferdinand's expression, though he seemed ill at ease.

"Don't you know where Bernard is?" he asked, turning to Nicole.

"He'll surely phone me tomorrow morning, and when I tell him what's happened he'll take the first plane . . ."

"What would you like us to do meanwhile?"

"I don't know . . . It's you who ought to make the necessary arrangements."

"What arrangements?"

"Your father was rich . . . First of all, there's the business, which is worth a lot of money."

Antoine turned red. Although the remark was meant for him personally, he did not want to answer.

"Half of the business belongs to Antoine, who was our father's partner for twenty years," declared Ferdinand.

"Are there any papers that were signed in the presence of a notary?"

"Not in the presence of a notary . . . They signed an agreement between themselves."

"And your father received half the profits every year?"

This time the judge did not answer for his brother.

"I paid him his share regularly."

"That means a big sum?"

"A certain sum, yes . . ."

"How much, for example?"

"One would have to look at the books."

"And where are the books?"

Antoine pointed to a modern commode with three doors. "They're here."

But he did not offer to show them to her.

"What did he do with the money?"

"That was his own affair. He didn't talk about it to anyone."

"All the same, he didn't keep it in his apartment?"

"I suppose not."

"Haven't you tried to find out?"

"No . . ."

He looked at Fernande, who was boiling inwardly and biting her nails so as not to lose her temper.

Why didn't Ferdinand say something to defend his brother? Both he and his wife had become speechless. The father had died at about ten o'clock, and at one in the morning, there they were, above his head, involved in a discussion about his money.

Antoine stood up and, mastering himself, declared in a trembling voice, "I prefer that you come and see . . ."

Ferdinand made a gesture of protest, though without conviction. His wife stood up before he did. Nicole first finished her cup of coffee and then walked to the door.

"Aren't you coming with us?" Antoine asked Fernande.

"I don't have the heart to."

Yet Fernande had been a streetwalker who wandered at night from bar to bar and whom Antoine had literally picked up in the street.

It was three years before he dared introduce her to his father. Then, after his marriage, although they had rented the apartment on the second floor, it was two years before his mother had said a word to her and allowed her to show her face on the ground floor.

They went down the ill-lit staircase in Indian file. The worn steps creaked beneath their feet. The door was not locked. In the living room, Madame Ledru, whom they had never called by her first name because, being the widow of a surveyor, she stood on her dignity, hastily got up from the couch on which she had been dozing.

The door of the bedroom was open, and one could see the quivering flames of the candles. They walked in without a word. Véronique crossed herself. Nicole merely gazed silently at the dead man's face.

"I don't know whether you want to look around in this room," said Antoine in a low voice.

Nicole's only answer was to withdraw to the living room. Ferdinand and his wife followed her. The room gave one the feeling that the clock had been turned back forty years. In a gilded frame above the fringed couch, an enlarged photograph of Victor Mature, the day laborer of Saint-Hippolyte, looked at them with expressionless eyes. A green plant—which one would have sworn was the same that had been there when the brothers were children—loomed above a copper jardiniere.

"I suppose these are the drawers that interest you."

"I haven't asked for anything," replied Nicole. "I merely think it's better all around that things be done properly."

There was an old dining-room buffet, the upper doors of which were fitted with leaded glass. Antoine opened its two drawers, revealing a jumble of small objects that had accumulated over the years.

A cardboard box contained photographs of the three brothers at different ages, a silver thimble, and a lock of hair that meant nothing to anyone there. Was it the hair of one of the children that the mother had wrapped in a piece of tissue paper? Was it a lock of her own hair that Auguste had cut off when they were engaged or in the early days of their marriage?

Two marbles, an agate, and a whistle. Newspaper articles praising the restaurant. Letters. Ferdinand recognized his own handwriting and Bernard's. There were also letters that Véronique had written from La Rochelle and later from Poitiers when her husband was too busy, some of which contained photos of their two children, Marie-Laure and Jean-Loup.

Marie-Laure was now living with a girl friend on Avenue Victor Hugo, where the two young women ran a women's novelty shop, and Jean-Loup was an intern at the Salpêtrière.

Old bills for pieces of furniture and for objects that no longer existed, and also Ferdinand's first high school report card.

"You see . . . no will . . . no money either in this drawer . . ."

He opened the one on the left. It was fuller than the first and overflowing with photos and letters. The photos were of people they hardly knew or did not know at all, of their mother's cousins, of childhood friends, of a class in a school playground. And then some little sachets containing hair and with the name of each of the brothers written in pencil.

In the bottom of the buffet were a few books, some balls of wool, and, on the lowest shelf, odds and ends of cloth of various colors that Eugénie Mature had preciously saved.

The top of the buffet contained glasses and a few bottles of liquor.

There was no desk in the apartment.

"There's still my parents' bedroom . . ."

They hesitated as he walked ahead, but they finally followed him. He opened the tall wardrobe and its drawers, and then a commode, which contained only linens.

There was no point in staying there. When they were on the landing, where they were crowded, they did not know whether they ought to go up or down.

"I've got to get my coat," said Nicole.

They went upstairs in silence. The visitors put on their hats and coats. Ferdinand would have liked to stay behind so as to dissociate himself from Bernard's common-law wife, but he was not asked to.

"I hope Bernard will be here tomorrow . . . I apologize for this visit . . . I was obliged to come . . ."

She was not asked why she was obliged, and she walked to the landing.

"See you tomorrow, Antoine," said Ferdinand. "I don't know at what time I'll be able to drop by. Ring me up at my office if you need me. I'll be there almost all day."

Véronique made an effort to kiss Fernande, something she had not done more than three or four times in her life.

"Ferdinand worries me. He overworks. He takes his profession so much to heart . . ."

When the door was finally closed and there was the sound of footsteps going down the stairs, Antoine and Fernande found themselves face to face. A long time went by without their saying a word. Antoine went into the bedroom and undressed. His wife picked up the cups and put them into the kitchen sink.

As she walked by the bathroom, she saw him, in his pajamas, brushing his teeth. She merely sighed, "We're in for something!"

He made no comment but simply asked, "Have you wound the clock?"

It was she who attended to the matter every day. The alarm rang at five in the morning. He would immediately turn it off, with a gesture that had become mechanical, and would get out of bed noiselessly, for Fernande still had two hours to sleep.

"The thing that disappoints me is Ferdinand's behavior . . . I didn't expect him to side with her."

Antoine did not answer. His brother had not sided outright with Nicole. Rather, he had remained neutral. It was because of his wife. If Véronique had said nothing, it was because she knew what attitude her husband would adopt.

"Good night," he sighed.

"Good night, Antoine."

There was an empty space in the bed between them. Now there was emptiness everywhere.

"Do you think Antoine knows where your father put his money?"

Ferdinand did not answer immediately. Settled in the seat beside his wife, who was driving, he stared blankly at the empty streets on the way to the Porte d'Orléans. He was glum and ill at ease.

34

He was upset by what had just happened, and he foresaw other difficulties.

"My father never talked about such things," he finally murmured.

Véronique was his wife, but she was not a Mature who had been born and bred in the old house on Rue de la Grande-Truanderie.

All his life, Auguste had been a jovial man with a hearty voice and ready wit, but he had also been a shrewd and secretive peasant who kept certain things to himself.

Did his wife herself know how much they made when the two of them ran the business?

He was the man, the head of the family. He could just as well have been the chief of a tribe who was surrounded by his children, daughters-in-law, and grandchildren.

If he had not tried to keep Ferdinand at home, it was because he had realized that his son would not stay. From the time he started going to school, the youngster was ashamed of the restaurant and of his father, and when he was asked what his father did for a living, he would answer, "He's in business."

It was the same when he was in high school. Ferdinand did not have the build of the Matures either. He was the puniest of the three sons, a dreamy, introspective boy.

He had never really been involved in the family life, and his youth had been a period of marking time until he left home.

He had not felt that he had a definite vocation. He had chosen law because two of his friends were in law school, but he soon realized that he was not meant for pleading, that his shyness was a handicap at the bar.

It was not exactly shyness. He looked at everything with a

desire to understand, as if seeking his rightful place among men.

"After all, he must have put his money somewhere."

"I know . . ."

"What amazes me is that none of you ever dared to ask him . . . You're his sons . . ."

Obviously! Antoine, perhaps, might have been able to. Ferdinand felt a certain affection for Antoine, who nevertheless resembled him so little. With Antoine, old Auguste had succeeded. Instead of going on with his studies, Antoine learned the business, while Bernard took advantage, as it were, of the war and enlisted in the army when he was eighteen.

He served only six months, the time it took the Germans to reach Paris, and thereafter he never lived in the family home.

"You think he put a lot of money aside?"

"He must have made quite a pile, and he spent hardly anything."

"Antoine was his favorite, wasn't he?"

"He's the one who stayed with him."

The others had urged him to sell his business, either to Antoine or someone else, and to retire to Auvergne with his wife. The old man would not hear of it. He needed his tin bar, his marble-topped tables, the coming and going that began in the early hours of the morning. He needed coffee and croissants, bottles of wine, the smell of cooking.

"Wasn't he capable of leaving his nest egg to Antoine without saying anything to anyone?"

"I don't think so."

"What's to be done if nothing is found?"

"I don't know yet."

36

Ferdinand was not rich. He had only his salary to live on. Five years before, his wife and he had done something rash. Was it she who was the more guilty of the two? Although the idea had been hers, he had not resisted, at any rate not enough.

Ever since their marriage, they had lived in old houses, at first in La Rochelle, then in Poitiers, and after that in Paris, where they had a third-floor apartment in a house without an elevator on Rue Saint-Louis-en-l'Île.

The two children were still living with them. Marie-Laure was taking courses in art history, and Jean-Loup had begun to study medicine.

The apartment had become too small for four adults, and there was only one bathroom for the whole family, a bathroom with an ancient hot-water tank.

Garden cities were beginning to be built on the outskirts of Paris, modern apartment buildings that were called *Résidences,* and almost every week Véronique showed her husband pictures of the new apartments that appeared in the newspapers.

"There's even a swimming pool!" exclaimed Jean-Loup.

The apartments were not for rent but for sale.

"After the first payment and the ten annual payments, there's no more rent to pay."

They had visited several of them on Sundays. What they saw did not always correspond to the description in the advertisement, but Véronique got enthusiastic over the *Résidence* of Sceaux Park.

They had waited six months for the house to be finished. Finally, each of them had his own bathroom. A terrace looked out on the landscape, and a swimming pool was at the disposal of the residents of the five buildings.

Ferdinand had bathed in it only twice, for he felt self-conscious about his poor build and did not have full control of his body. He could hardly swim, and it made him feel ashamed. Véronique, who thought she was too stout, did not bathe in the pool either.

"We'll be able to do without a maid," she had said. "Everything works by electricity."

They had actually done without a maid for seven or eight months, but as Véronique had to act as chauffeur, they ended by hiring one.

Marie-Laure, at the age of twenty-two, was the first to leave. The reason she gave was that she wanted to earn her living. She had become infatuated with a girl friend, and they had opened a shop together. Her parents hardly ever saw her. She lived in another world and no longer had anything in common with them.

Thus, a room remained unoccupied, although her parents kept Marie-Laure's furniture in it, out of a kind of superstition, as if she were going to come back.

When she did set foot in the apartment, it was almost always to get things that belonged to her. Little by little she emptied the room, and Ferdinand resigned himself to using it as a study.

And now a second room was empty, for Jean-Loup lived almost entirely at the Salpêtrière, where he was an intern.

He was an odd boy, unobtrusive and timid, like his father, and perhaps a bit moody. He had decided to specialize in child psychiatry. He, too, wore glasses. His fellow students regarded him as an ambitious young man who was interested only in his studies.

Studies that were expensive. Marie-Laure had also needed a lot of money when she set up her shop.

Installments had to be paid on the apartment, and interest accumulated.

The situation was not tragic. Other families had the same difficulties. Ferdinand could not claim that he was unwell. He was never really sick. It was a matter of twinges, sore throats, pains in the joints, stomach-aches, ailments which, without worrying him, made him anxious, and Véronique, who was going through her menopause, was not very helpful.

With the father's money, they would be saved. Their share would be enough to pay what they owed on the apartment, and they would no longer have to bother about installments.

They would be able to buy a new car, for theirs had already done more than sixty thousand miles, and to travel when they were on vacation instead of spending two or three weeks at a second-class hotel in Brittany.

"I don't know whether you feel as I do . . . Antoine didn't seem to me to be acting natural. He was ill at ease, as if he were hiding something from us."

When Ferdinand was fifteen and Antoine twelve, they got on very well, and Antoine would confide in Ferdinand, whom he admired very much.

"You have an easier time of it in school than I! You're lucky to be smart."

Ferdinand would encourage him.

"You're smart too. Maybe it's another kind of smartness."

It was odd to think that there had been real intimacy between them and that for years they had slept in the same bed.

Yet that evening they had hardly dared look each other in the face.

"I mistrust Fernande too. In the first place, why did they wait two hours before phoning us? He was your father, wasn't he? You're the oldest. You're the one who should have taken things in hand."

They had arrived. The building had a garage in which there were smarter and more powerful cars than theirs.

They took the elevator. There, too, they lived on the third floor. Véronique, who had the key in her bag, opened the door and put on the light.

The house in the Market area had a smell that one recognized immediately after being away for months. But there was nothing of the sort here. Everything was clean and orderly. They had had to buy new furniture, for the old things, which had followed them in their various homes, clashed with the setting.

"Is your throat still sore?"

"A little."

They went straight to the bedroom, where once again they were going to undress in each other's presence.

The two brothers had also undressed in each other's presence when they were young, and yet they now felt like strangers.

Wasn't Véronique a stranger to him? Their common memories dated only from their first meeting at the home of a fellow student. She was the daughter of an important commercial lawyer, and her family had lived on Boulevard Haussmann at a time when the neighborhood was one of the smartest in Paris.

The husband and wife did not have the same past, and words conjured up different images for them.

They had been in love. They had thought so. They had

certainly been in love, for they had got married and had lived together ever since.

It had never occurred to Ferdinand to deceive his wife or, with all the more reason, to leave her.

They had had two children. They had known happy hours, particularly when Jean-Loup and then Marie-Laure were born. The christenings and first communions had been occasions for lively gatherings.

When they had moved into the new apartment, the four of them had walked all around it with delight. They had drunk champagne, convinced that cares and troubles were gone forever.

Ferdinand worked very hard. He was scrupulously thorough, a perfectionist. The file of a judicial inquiry had almost to be wrested from his hands because it was never complete enough for him.

Only in his office did he feel a certain superiority. Men and women, all of whom were more or less "cases," marched in and out.

He would observe them with his nearsighted eyes and ask them questions in an effort to understand. Unlike certain colleagues, he did not regard them as enemies of society, and some of them intimidated him because they had a strength of character which he knew that he himself lacked.

In a few hours, tired after an almost sleepless night, he would again be face to face with René Mauvis, who would be handcuffed. The corridor would be full of reporters and photographers, as it had been every day for two weeks.

In the late afternoon he could not even send Mauvis back to Santé Prison lest the crowd attack him, and he therefore kept him in a cell in the basement of the courthouse.

What did he know about Mauvis? Until the age of thirty-two he had been a model and unassuming clerk in a mid-town bank and had lived alone in a three-room apartment on Rue de Turenne, near Place des Vosges.

Mauvis was a bachelor. His concierge had never seen him come home with a woman, and as far as his colleagues knew, he had no girl friends.

His only passion seemed to be billiards, which he played two or three evenings a week in a café on Boulevard Beaumarchais. He was accused of having strangled two little boys, within a period of six months, in Saint-Germain Forest, where he claimed he had never in his life been.

"Can't you take a day off and rest? You're practically alone in court on Saturday."

It was true. He was allowed to carry on the investigation in his own way and at times of his own choice. He was tempted. It was essential that he have a talk with Antoine the next day, or rather that same day, and perhaps with Bernard too, if he came back from the Riviera.

"Are you hungry?"

"No."

"Do you want a pill?"

She was referring to the sleeping pills that he took.

"I don't think I need it . . . Good night."

They kissed. It was a ritual gesture before turning over and going to sleep. Each was used to the other's smell, to the smell of the couple, and they had reached the point of breathing in the same rhythm.

The father was dead. Ferdinand used to see him not more than once a month, when he dropped in, on his way by, to drink a cup of coffee at the bar.

"Won't you have lunch with us?"

He would sometimes let himself be tempted, would recapture the taste of the cooking of former days, but he usually refused because he was not allowed to pay.

The father was dead, and there was suddenly a great void.

III

Antoine dressed quietly in the semidarkness. He knew that Fernande heard him anyway, but he did not speak to her so as not to wake her completely.

In another month it would be broad daylight when he began his marketing. In the heart of Paris, he followed the succession of the seasons by the hour of sunrise, just as one did in the country.

He put on a turtleneck sweater and an old black leather jacket. On the first floor, he opened the door of his parents' apartment. Madame Ledru was sleeping on the couch in the living room. The light of the candles was dancing in the room where Auguste was alone with eternity.

There had been no vigil. Nobody had kept the dead man company, and Antoine felt somewhat guilty about it.

On Rue Pierre-Lescot, the air was already heavy with the smell of vegetables, and a special light shone on the dark little men who were moving busily about heaps of food in the iron sheds.

Most of them had been there since the night before. The dawn was cool, and women were slapping their arms in order to warm themselves. In the bars, coffee, white wine, and brandy were being served without letup, as they had been in his restaurant in the old days.

"Hello," he called out as he went by.

He did not know all the names, but the faces were familiar to him.

"Hello, Antoine," people would answer, especially the old ones who had known him as a child, when he went with his father. There were also some from the neighborhood who had played with him in the street.

The others would say, more respectfully, "Hello, Monsieur Antoine."

A toothless vegetable woman, who was wearing a man's jacket over two or three sweaters, asked, "Is it true?"

"It's true, Berthe."

"He always used to say to me that he'd die behind his bar."

He saw the first strawberries in pretty baskets of woven shavings, and he discussed the price before buying twenty baskets of them.

"I'll send them over in a little while with Nestor. I also have peaches, but of course they're not from Auvergne."

He continued on his way, at first among the pyramids of fruit and vegetables that rose up in the streets, and then in the passageways of the sheds.

He had his dealers. He needed flowers for the tables and chose anemones. Then he went back and bought several bunches of chrysanthemums for the death chamber.

The darkness was fading, and the big lamps were getting paler above people's heads. As he walked along, the menus took shape in his mind, almost mechanically.

"I was told about your poor father . . ."

Or else it was:

"Who'd have thought that old Auguste would go off so suddenly! . . . After all, it's better that way . . . He was so proud of his strength that he'd have been ashamed of being sick."

The whole little world of the Market had heard the news, and even those who said nothing to Antoine looked at him more solemnly than usual.

He was going to have to attend to the funeral, but he did not want to do anything before consulting his two brothers. In the past they had been relieved by Antoine's staying with their parents, because it had spared them a responsibility.

Now that Auguste was dead, they would not at all relish their brother's behaving as if he were specially privileged.

It had already started the night before. Even Nicole, who was not really a member of the family, had come running to defend Bernard's rights.

As for Ferdinand, his attitude had not been clear, and probably he would not side with Antoine when the time came.

Yet, of the three, Antoine had been the least lucky, for he had wasted four long years in a camp in Pomerania.

Ferdinand had not been called up because of his nearsightedness. He had spent the war years in La Rochelle, where he had just received an appointment.

As for Bernard, he had regained his freedom after spending six months in uniform far from the front.

It was not Antoine who had proposed to their father that he stay with him. He could have worked a few years more at the Strasbourg Tavern or elsewhere and have put aside enough money to set up on his own in any neighborhood. He was hard-working and knew his job.

If he had been willing to stay, perhaps it was so that there would always be a Mature on Rue de la Grande-Truanderie.

Even when they were very young, the two others had wanted to get away from home, but not he, and it was not, as one might have thought, because he was worried about the future.

He felt at home in the little restaurant with its good smells. He had thought about it constantly when he was in Germany and wondered whether he would live to see the end of the war.

His father sent him packages, and his mother postcards, which were full of mistakes and which he answered without ever admitting that he was depressed or that he suffered periodically from dysentery.

"Well, are you staying?"

"I am," he answered with a smile.

What happened that day was quite unexpected. They were both standing on the threshold at about seven in the morning. It was in May. The spring was particularly lovely.

The moment before, they were still a father and son standing next to each other and watching the traffic in the street.

But the moment Antoine gave his answer, the relationship between the two men changed. As naturally as can be, they became partners, accomplices of a sort, and the difference in age ceased to exist.

"Do you agree that this is the right time to expand?"

"We ought to take advantage of the new clientele as soon as possible."

"The apartment on the second floor is going to be free. The Meyers are going back to Alsace."

The Meyers, the Chaves, little Madame Brossier, the Maniages, the Gagneaus, the Allards, Justine and Berthe, and hundreds of others were not only names to them but faces, real persons who had entered their lives at one time or another.

Some had gone away, leaving only a faint trace. Others were still around and had greeted Auguste's son solemnly that morning.

To them he was the old man's heir. To them, but not to his brothers, nor to his sister-in-law, nor to Nicole.

The father and son did not even realize how it had happened. At first, while they were discussing plans for enlarging the restaurant, Antoine had replaced his mother at the stove and had added new dishes to the restaurant's specialties.

The customers got used to him. Wearing his white chef's cap, he would come and shake hands with them when his father asked him to.

"Come in for a minute. Monsieur Bicard wants to meet you."

He would dry his hands on his apron, and Auguste was proud to say, as he turned to the tall, broad-shouldered young man, "This is my son Antoine. He's now my partner."

Actually, it was not yet a real partnership. His father would give him whatever money he needed, as when he was an adolescent.

"What did you make at the Strasbourg Tavern? I'll give you twice as much."

The old man made the offer several months later, and at that time the other brothers saw no objection.

The idea of the glass partition between the inner room and the kitchen was Antoine's. A friend had spoken to him about the same kind of thing in a Milanese restaurant.

Joseph, who had already been working in the restaurant

before the war, had wisecracked, "The clients'll look as if they were at a sideshow."

That was why the back room had since been called the Sideshow, when it was not the Senate. As for the first room, with its tin bar and old-fashioned marble-topped tables, they eventually christened it, because of its past, the Flea Market.

"Attend to the Fleas. I'll wait on the Sideshow."

The customers, of course, suspected nothing, just as they did not know the nicknames by which old Joseph referred to some of them.

A cabinet minister who came for lunch at least once a week would have been surprised to learn that he was referred to as the Mug, and one of the leading society women in Paris would have had a stroke if she had known that on Rue de la Grande-Truanderie she was vulgarly called the Hag.

When Antoine met Fernande, he was still living with his parents and was on a salary. His mother kept house. He slept in the bedroom which was later given to Madame Ledru.

Fernande was very young and delicate-looking and was lost in a world of which she understood nothing. She had left her Breton village a few months before, and after a few evenings in a dance hall on Rue de Lappe found herself walking the streets.

It took him some time to realize that he loved her, and only then did he make her change her way of life. He rented a room for her in a hotel on Rue Étienne-Marcel where he joined her every night.

Because he was the only one of the sons who still lived with his parents, his mother could not get used to the idea that he had become a man, and she was upset about his sleeping away from home.

"You ought to get married, Antoine. There are lots of nice girls in the neighborhood. You'd have no trouble finding one. I'm sure that Marie Chaussard . . ."

The Chaussards were their neighbors. They were butchers. The father had come to Paris at about the same time as Auguste, and the two of them had set up in business within a year of each other.

Marie was plump and rosy, like most women who live in a butcher shop, a fact that Antoine had often noticed, though without knowing how to explain it.

She was a little younger than he. Her brother Léon worked with his father and at six in the morning was already cutting up animals behind the closed grating of the shop.

Antoine did not marry Marie Chaussard but, three years later, Fernande, and his mother had cried. Then he waited for the apartment on the second floor to be free so that he could move into it.

His brothers knew almost nothing about their life, which they had seen only from the outside. As far as they were concerned, Antoine had married a trollop who led him by the nose.

Later, they were obliged to recognize that the trollop wasn't such a bad wife after all.

As for Antoine, he regretted only one thing: that he did not have children. The reason was that Fernande had contracted a venereal disease a few weeks after coming to Paris and had had to have an operation.

He could not forgive the doctors for having literally butchered her. As for her, after so many years she was still ashamed to let him see her naked belly.

"That's life," as François, the redheaded waiter, would

say, he who at the age of thirty-five had five children and whose wife was expecting a sixth.

François would have been satisfied with one or two, at most three.

He had been obliged to move to Romainville, near a quarry, so as to have room enough for his kids.

"That's life."

At present, the one-time trollop would go upstairs several times a day to take care of her mother-in-law, who was no longer aware of what was going on. Sunk in her bed or armchair, the old lady lived in a kind of dream world, and God knows what the life around her meant to her.

She would sometimes smile vaguely, the way babies do, or clutch hold of Madame Ledru's arm when she was seized with an indefinable fear.

She had become so thin that she seemed unearthly. She did not suffer. She lived in a world of her own and recognized none of the people around her.

In a little while, Jojo, the Market idiot, who had inordinately large hands, would be bringing to the restaurant the crates and bags he had picked up in the sheds of Antoine's various dealers.

Antoine, who had come back to Rue de la Grande-Truanderie, entered Léon Chaussard's butcher shop by the small door.

Léon was two years older than he and had four butcher shops in Paris. He, too, had stayed at home with his father. At the age of eighty-three the old man still made his round of the sheds every morning.

In the afternoon, when a ray of sun brightened the sidewalk in front of the shop, the old man would install himself on a chair and sit there an hour or two smoking his pipe slowly and watching people go by.

"What do you advise today?"

"I have some nice sweetbread, not too expensive."

"Let me have fifteen portions . . . Do you have lamb chops?"

"Not the kind you like."

Antoine fingered the meats, made his choice, and changed his menus accordingly.

"Is it true that it happened right in the restaurant?"

"Yes."

"Did he realize he was dying?"

"I don't know. He fell to the floor and seemed to have lost consciousness immediately. One of his eyes was shut. He had trouble breathing. I wonder whether, in cases like that, the mind keeps working. Dr. Patin claims it doesn't."

"Does your mother know?"

Antoine shrugged.

"You know how she is."

"After all, it's better for her."

Perhaps for Auguste too, since he would not have to bury his wife. He had not spent a single night away from her ever since they had been married, and even in recent times, when she looked at him as if he were a stranger or pet dog, he would often sit down in front of her in the hope that they might pick up the thread of God knows what conversation.

"Have your brothers come?"

"Only Ferdinand. We weren't able to notify Bernard. He's out of town."

Léon had two sisters, one of whom was the Marie whom the family had wanted to marry off to Antoine. Both girls were married, Marie to someone who worked in the Tax Department. Léon had had trouble with his two brothers-in-law when he had taken over the father's business.

"Did Ferdinand say anything?"

They understood each other without having to go into detail.

"Nicole was the one who talked most."

"Did Bernard finally marry her?"

"No, but it's as if he did. Last night you'd have thought she was demanding on behalf of the family that I give an accounting."

"Do you have things in writing?"

"Only a letter from my father in which he recognizes that I'm half-owner of the business."

"Signed before a notary?"

"Not at all. My father consulted what he called his business counselor, a kind of consultant who had a small office on Rue Coquillière."

"Do you know him?"

"I saw him two or three times, when he came to eat in the restaurant. That was long ago. A dirty, sloppy-looking fellow who was always carrying a black leather briefcase . . . Jason, I think . . . yes, Ernest Jason."

"Is he a lawyer?"

"No . . . As far as I know, he's a former business agent who got into trouble. My father had complete confidence in him because his family was from Riom."

"Do you think your brothers'll make you sell or buy up their share?"

"Anything can happen . . . Especially as far as the two wives are concerned . . . Last night, my sister-in-law, who'd always refused to speak to Nicole, sided with her."

"You'd better not do anything without seeing a lawyer, someone serious, who knows about business."

They did not shake hands. They had known each other too long.

"So long, Léon."

"Good luck."

It was after seven. The shutters of the restaurant were raised, and Jules, who was wearing a blue apron and whose sleeves were rolled up, had started the coffee.

On the counter was a basket of warm croissants and near it a pyramid of hard-boiled eggs in a wire container.

"Morning, boss."

Antoine went behind the counter to get a cup of coffee. He ate three croissants, then, after hesitating briefly, a hard-boiled egg. At a table were two truck gardeners who had taken thick slices of buttered bread out of their pockets and were drinking white wine.

"Has my wife come down?"

"Not yet."

"Has anyone phoned?"

That was the hour when he went up to wash and change. Then, when the chef arrived, the two of them would draw up the menus for lunch and dinner.

Only two or three dishes ever changed, and the day's specials were written in red on the big bill of fare.

The other dishes, from the *cochonnades* to the *flangarde*, a kind of cold custard, remained unchanged.

"Has the bread been delivered?"

He had just noticed that only three loaves were left in the window.

"If my brother comes, let me know."

"The judge?"

To everyone, including the family, Ferdinand was the judge.

"My son, the judge," as Auguste had said only the night before.

He had been proud of him. There had been, as it were, no bonds between them, but Ferdinand was nevertheless a son of his who had become a magistrate.

Antoine was a man like himself. They understood each other. They shared the same kind of life, had the same way of thinking, lived among the same people.

At times, when Auguste had taken a little drink at the table of an old customer, his son would whisper, "Remember what the doctor told you."

"I only wet my lips. After all, I can't refuse to have a drink with friends."

He had been a little afraid of Antoine. The way his son looked at him from a distance when he had a glass in his hand made him feel uncomfortable. He would sometimes cheat, would pour himself a glass of wine at the bar when Jules was elsewhere for a moment. He imagined that no one would know.

Antoine had not been urged by Fernande to speak to his father. It had been his own idea. He had had to brace himself, as if he were doing something wrong.

"Papa, we've got to have a serious talk."

Words like that were almost unimaginable in a home where life seemed to follow the rhythm of nature, to unfold without complications, without real problems.

"About what, son?"

It was about 11 A.M., a time of day when things were slack. They had sat down in the Sideshow. Behind the partition Julien Bernu was bustling about with his assistant, Arthur's predecessor, for Arthur was only seventeen at the time. Nor had they yet taken on Big Louise to peel the vegetables.

"I'm now thirty . . . I'm married . . . I could be a father."

"Is your wife pregnant?"

"No. The doctor says she can't have children."

"Is that what you want to talk to me about?"

"I want to talk to you about my situation in the restaurant."

"I understand," said Auguste, whose face clouded over.

And silencing his son with a gesture, he added, "If I were in your place, I'd do the very same thing. It's natural for you to think of the future."

"I enjoy working with you," mumbled Antoine, lowering his head. "But what if . . ."

"Yes, what if I should die. Your two brothers would demand their share of the restaurant, where they've never done anything."

Auguste had lit one of the small, very dark cigars that he smoked from time to time.

"You're right. We ought to straighten that out. I'll have to take it up with my counselor."

He had not proposed that he discuss the matter with Ferdinand. Yet, in his mind, the word "counselor" covered lawyers, judges, and notaries as well as business agents and advisers.

It was the first time in the seventeen years since that conversation had taken place that Antoine realized the full consequences of it.

The two men had let weeks go by without referring to the matter again. Then, one afternoon, when Antoine returned to the restaurant after his nap, his father handed him an envelope.

"Read this agreement and tell me whether it'll do."

Antoine went upstairs again, almost furtively, to read it.

"What is it?" asked Fernande.

"A business matter."

"Anything wrong?"

The paper began as follows: "I the undersigned, Auguste Victor André Mature, born in Saint-Hippolyte, Puy-de-Dôme, on July 25, 1887 . . ."

Antoine reread the date twice. It seemed to him so long ago!

". . . owner of a business establishment known as The Auvergnat, on Rue de la Grande-Truanderie . . ."

His father had diligently copied a text that had been written for him and by virtue of which he recognized that in exchange for his son's investing a certain amount in the business and of his working in it, the restaurant henceforth belonged to the two men. The net profits, after the annual inventory, were to be shared equally.

Antoine had shown the paper to Ferdinand a few days later.

"What do you think of it?"

"Who drafted the agreement?"

"Someone Papa knows and whom he trusts. Why do you ask? Anything wrong with it?"

"It's no great shakes, but, all in all, it'll do. Have you really put money into the business?"

"All my savings."

Ferdinand had looked at him ironically.

"You're lucky to have been able to save. It's obvious you don't have children."

"I'll have to tell Bernard about it."

"That'll encourage him to drop in and hit you for a loan more often."

Time had flown by! Those conversations seemed to have taken place only yesterday, and yet the restaurant had had time to win its two-star rating in the Michelin Guidebook; Marie-Laure, who could have been married and a mother, had declared her independence and was running a shop; Auguste had just died; and their mother was practically no longer in the world of the living.

Had Antoine done the right thing in countersigning the paper that his father had handed him one afternoon with a serious look, and perhaps reluctantly?

When Antoine came down again an hour later, a half-dozen customers were standing at the bar and others were sitting at tables. It was the morning clientele, people from the Market and from the neighborhood. They were all talking about what had happened the night before, and when Antoine entered there was a sudden silence.

"Hasn't my brother come?" he asked Jules in a tone of surprise.

"He went up to the first floor," answered Jules, who was rinsing glasses at the bar.

Antoine was freshly shaven and was wearing a dark suit, as he usually did. He went up to the first floor and opened the door, which was never locked so that Madame Ledru would not be needlessly disturbed. Besides, what was the use of locking it?

His mother was already settled in her armchair near the

window, the muslin curtain of which was drawn so that she could see what was going on in the street.

Madame Ledru, who had found time to wash and dress, was giving her lunch. She kept dipping little pieces of buttered bread into a soft-boiled egg and then putting the edge of the spoon to the old woman's lips.

"Are you looking for Monsieur Ferdinand? He's at the back."

Antoine found him standing at the foot of the bed in which their father was lying and on both sides of which fresh candles were burning.

Ferdinand, who was standing and staring at the dead man's face, from which the towel had been removed, looked as if he were praying. Was he really praying? Had Véronique, who attended mass every Sunday and abstained from meat on Friday, converted him?

The two brothers remained standing in silence for several moments. Their eyes were looking in the same direction, and perhaps they felt again, during those few seconds, the bonds that had existed between them when they were children.

Ferdinand was the first to move toward the door. Antoine followed him. Neither of them stopped in the dark living room, where they did not feel they belonged. They went downstairs and sat down at a table in the second room, which was empty.

"Didn't Véronique come with you?"

"She dropped me off at the door. She took advantage of being in the neighborhood to buy a few things at the Market."

She had obviously wanted to leave the two brothers together—or perhaps it was Ferdinand's idea.

"Have you heard from Bernard?"

"Not yet."

"Do you really think Nicole doesn't know where he is?"

"It's hard to tell with her."

Bernard was one of Ferdinand's big worries, for he had the unfortunate habit of getting involved in rather shady affairs, and several times he had signed checks that were not covered. Their father or one of the brothers had always fixed things up, but there was a limit to what could be done, and Ferdinand's professional situation might one day become delicate.

"What was he like the last time you saw him?"

"He was wearing a new suit and had a broad smile. He was setting up a company to sell television programs in foreign countries."

Bernard had spells of euphoria during which he dressed smartly and assumed the manner of an important businessman. He would refer to well-known people, saying that they were his partners, and listening to him, one got the impression that they were on intimate terms.

"I had dinner yesterday with the Secretary of Commerce, who told . . ."

The astonishing thing was that it was not always false. He was sometimes seen at Fouquet's, Maxim's, the Berkeley, and, in the evening, in the fashionable night clubs.

On Sundays he managed to get himself invited to private estates in the outlying suburbs, and usually he had a car. Did it belong to him or had he borrowed it from a friend?

"Do you believe it, about that deal?" asked Antoine, who had a certain respect for his elder brother's opinions.

"Same as the others."

After a few weeks, there would be no further mention of

the matter. Bernard would turn up in low spirits, with his features drawn and a shifty look in his eyes:

"Listen, Ferdinand, you simply must help me out. It'll be the last time. If you let me have five thousand, I'll be able to wait for a big sum of money that's coming in, and I'll pay you back. Besides, there's always my share of the inheritance as a guarantee."

Was it entirely his fault? When he was discharged from the army, immediately after the invasion, the black market was beginning, and Bernard found a way of making money.

He would get a barrel of nails for a provincial hardware dealer, who would give him in exchange a number of whole hams, which he then sold at a high price. Everything was scarce. Anything could be turned to account. It was simply a matter of knowing where to get merchandise, which became a medium of exchange.

He kept his ears open in the bars he frequented, and this enabled him to act as intermediary in important deals.

"What of it?" he would say. "What's wrong with what I'm doing? Isn't my father involved in deals too? If it weren't for the black market, Paris would have died of hunger long ago."

It was precisely about Bernard that Ferdinand wanted to talk.

"It would surprise me very much if Bernard didn't show up today. Nicole must have spoken to him by now about the inheritance."

"I'm not to blame if Father didn't leave a will."

"Bernard won't think so."

"Do you?"

"Maybe we haven't searched carefully enough. He may also have left it with a notary, or in a vault in some bank.

You who lived with him ought to know whether he went to a bank from time to time, in which case it's probably one in the neighborhood."

Antoine made no comment. He was incapable of answering and looked guilty, although he felt innocent.

"When did you give him his share of the profits?"

"Around the end of January, after the inventory."

"Was it a big sum?"

"Rather big."

"Did you pay by check?"

"No. In cash. Everything here in the Market is paid for in cash. The agents, the truck gardeners, the middlemen always have big wads of bills on them."

"Did he get his share at the end of January?"

"At the beginning of February . . . February third, to be exact."

"What did he do with it?"

"I have no idea . . . He went upstairs."

"We haven't found any money there."

"Maybe because we didn't look thoroughly enough, as you said. It's now March. He had time to take the money elsewhere."

"Did he ever tell you whether he bought property?"

"He didn't talk to me about his personal affairs. It wasn't for me to ask. Would *you* have dared ask him for an accounting?"

Ferdinand was forced to admit that he would not. Despite the fact that their father had aged and had sometimes been touchingly naïve, he nevertheless had remained head of the family, and he had made a point of letting everyone feel it.

"An idea occurred to me a little while ago, when I was talking to Léon."

"The butcher?"

"That's right . . . I was telling him about the paper that father and I once signed. It wasn't he who drew it up. He merely copied what someone had drafted for him. I think I know who. A certain Jason, Ernest Jason, who had an office on Rue Coquillière. He had lunch here two or three times. He was middle-aged at the time, with a yellow, bilious complexion. I don't know what's become of him, but I'll try to find out."

"It would be a good thing if we could talk to him before Bernard gets back."

It was odd the way both of them, especially Ferdinand, feared the youngest brother, the one who had almost gone to the bad.

"When is the funeral taking place?"

"I haven't thought about it yet . . . Tuesday?"

"Make it early, because I have a big day in court."

"It can't be earlier than nine o'clock."

"I suppose there'll be a prayer at the end?"

"I plan to attend to it this morning. First I have to see the undertaker."

"Are you going to send out announcements?"

Ferdinand quite naturally shifted the responsibility for these details onto his brother.

"It's absolutely essential."

"You won't be able to mention Nicole's name . . ."

"Of course not."

"One more question . . . Don't think I'm asking it out of personal interest . . . How much do you think the business is worth?"

"It depends . . . The government has definitely decided to transfer the Market to Rungis. Most of the old houses will be torn down, including this one and probably the whole street. Things'll drag on for a while, but it's obvious that in three years, at most, the new owner would have to break even. That being so, we'd be lucky to get more than a hundred thousand francs."

To Antoine, who handled big bills all day long, the figure seemed very low. But Ferdinand's involuntary reaction made him realize that his brother didn't think so.

"Judging from what you tell me, I suppose that during the last few years you must have given Father more than five hundred thousand francs. Is that right?"

"He certainly didn't have much less than a million."

"Bernard'll want to see the books."

"I'll show them to him."

"He'll go wild when he sees those figures."

"What can I do?"

Ferdinand looked at his watch and stood up.

"My wife must be waiting for me in the car . . . I'll let you attend to the funeral." And pointing to the ceiling, he added, "I'm planning to come to see him tomorrow, Sunday, with the children."

Just as he was leaving, he could not prevent himself from looking at Antoine admiringly and exclaiming, as if he were joking, "Say, you're rich!"

"I work . . ."

"So do I."

The old car was at the curb down the street, and Véronique was at the wheel.

"Has he found the will?"

"No. I don't think he spent much time looking for it. He mentioned a business agent with whom my father used to deal long ago. All he knows is that he had an office on Rue Coquillière."

She threaded her way between the trucks. The car was permeated with the smell of the vegetables and flowers she had bought.

Ferdinand realized that it would be wiser not to mention any figures to his wife, but he could not resist.

"Guess how much Antoine gave our father since they became partners."

"I have no idea . . . A lot?"

"Close to a million."

"Which means that Antoine too has a million. Is that right?"

"So it seems."

"We therefore ought to inherit more than three hundred thousand francs . . . not counting our share of the restaurant."

They looked at each other unbelievingly, torn between joy and fear. To them, who had to be careful about every expense, the figures were staggering.

They would have been ashamed to live on Rue de la Grande-Truanderie, which in the morning smelled of the Market and in the afternoon of poverty. Nor would they have been willing to go up and down the dark, worm-eaten stairway several times a day and to live in rooms which, even if they had been modernized, smacked of small shopkeepers. A butcher's shop on one side, a narrow dry-goods store on the other, and the hubbub of the Market all night long.

But Antoine had made a million!

"Do you think the money'll turn up?"

"It's bound to be somewhere."

"You who know your father, you ought to have some idea of what he might have done with it."

"During the war, he bought gold, he admitted it to me. I know he kept it in the house, but he never told me where. I don't know whether he continued . . . It's possible . . . It's also possible that he bought property . . . That's the kind of investment that tempts people like him."

They had reached the courthouse, and Ferdinand became the judge again. Briefcase in hand, he rushed to the main stairway, looking very preoccupied.

"My father died," he rapped out to the court clerk, who had been surprised to see him come late.

And the clerk did not know whether he ought to put out his hand to express his condolence.

"Send for Mauvis."

He really had to stop thinking about that million. The mention of it affected him almost like a blow in the solar plexus. He had never envied anyone, particularly not his brother, although Antoine was taller, younger, and better built than he.

A simple figure, mentioned in a very natural tone, had suddenly made him see Antoine in a different light.

Until that morning, Ferdinand, being the eldest, had somewhat considered himself head of the family. He was the most intelligent and most educated, and it seemed obvious to him that he had been more of a success than the others.

Of course, Antoine drove a more luxurious car than his, and every August, when the restaurant was closed, he and Fernande would travel to Venice, Greece, Spain, or elsewhere.

66

A thick folder had been prepared for him and was lying on his desk. In a few minutes the police would bring to his office a small, quiet-looking man who earned, at most, a thousand francs a month working all day in a bank.

Ferdinand suddenly felt inferior. Antoine had summoned up the image of wads of bank notes that were passed from hand to hand like ordinary merchandise. He remembered his amazement when, as a child, he had seen the business agents take similar rolls from their pockets while drinking their spiked coffee at the bar.

It had never occurred to him that Antoine was now in the same class.

"Has Brabant called from the police station?"

"He's following up on a new witness, but he doesn't think he can get hold of him today because of the weekend."

Would he resign if his father's million was found? He was thinking about it seriously, in spite of himself, while sharpening his pencil.

No! In the first place, his share wouldn't be enough to live on. It was better to wait until retirement age and get his full pension.

Besides, what would he do all day in his apartment in Sceaux? He had no small passions. He didn't potter around. He had never collected anything. He didn't go fishing or hunting.

Almost every evening he took files home to study while Véronique read or watched television in the next room.

As a matter of fact, what would he do with his time when he retired? Would they sell the apartment, which had already become too big and which was so expensive?

To go where? To the country? Neither Véronique nor he

cared for the country. A wasp was enough to frighten his wife, who had never wanted to go picnicking with the children because she loathed sitting on the grass.

He would read, well and good. He would go walking.

He suddenly felt as if he were naked, vulnerable. He had thought his life was normal, satisfactory, even enviable, and all at once he realized that there was nothing at the end of it.

Except, perhaps, if the million was found, a million which he had not earned, which came from elsewhere, from the patient work first of his father and mother in the restaurant of which he was ashamed, then of the old man and Antoine.

They, too, would travel, Véronique and he. They would spend part of the winter in the South, which they hardly knew. They had been there for short stays, but without enough money to live there as one should.

He was not accusing Antoine of cheating them. His brother had nevertheless profited from the family business. And he had been careful to have their father sign an agreement.

Of course, it had not been proven that the document was enough to establish his rights. Ferdinand had hardly ever bothered about common law, and even less about commercial law.

He looked at the first typewritten page of the file without seeing it. He heard someone coughing in front of him. It was one of the two policemen who had brought René Mauvis.

The round-shouldered, blank-looking prisoner was standing between the two men in uniform. Nothing in his attitude betrayed his impatience.

"Sit down."

He sat down on a chair, while the policemen installed themselves on a bench against the wall.

Ferdinand looked at his watch, as he had done when he was with his brother.

"Hasn't your lawyer come? Dubois, are you sure you sent for him?"

The clerk nodded. He, too, was a poor man. So were the policemen. They were waiting. A half hour later they would still be waiting, with the impersonal air of people who stand in line in front of a movie house, of those who stood in line in front of stores during the war.

Their father had indirectly benefited from the war. Thanks to the food he had managed to obtain, his clientele had changed. As a matter of fact, Antoine had benefited from the war too.

Bernard had never lived so well as at that time—which must have got him into bad habits. He was not unhappy. When he had money he spent it without compunction, and when he had none he borrowed shamelessly from his father or brothers.

"Call up his lawyer."

The clerk obeyed. A moment later his voice expressed surprise.

"Are you sure, Mademoiselle? Didn't he leave a message?"

The poor man was flabbergasted and hardly dared repeat to the judge what he had just learned.

"Monsieur Gerbois and his wife left last night for their country home near Dreux."

The others had come for nothing.

"Take him back."

Mauvis, who was still handcuffed, stood up docilely and walked out between the two policemen.

"You may go too, Dubois."

"Are you staying, sir?"

"I don't know . . . I'll see."

He had nothing to do and was not tempted to go home, where he had nothing to do either.

Finally, he took down his hat and coat and then turned around in the empty corridor to lock the door.

IV

It was half past twelve. The slanting sunlight lit up the front room, the Flea Market, as old Joseph called it, although the clientele had become much the same as in the Sideshow. The old tin counter now looked more like a stage prop than a real bar.

Fernande, who was wearing a black dress, had just lifted herself onto her high chair behind the cashier's desk, while Liselotte, who was in the cloakroom, pulled her skirt halfway up her thighs to readjust her garters.

There were still only about ten customers. Julien Bernu and his helpers were at their posts. Everyone was ready, as in the theater. It was somewhat like a play, with afternoon and evening performances. All the actors, major and minor, knew their roles by heart.

Antoine, in a dazzling shirt, was holding a parchmentlike bill of fare that Joseph—as usual—called the program. Antoine went over to a couple who were waiting to give their order.

Saturday had become a quiet day ever since important people had got into the habit of beginning the weekend on Friday. Even the streets of Paris had a different look.

When the front door opened, it was not a customer who came in, but Bernard Mature. He was wearing a camel's-hair coat and a beige hat.

He took two or three steps and remained standing in the

middle of the floor. Without even glancing at his sister-in-law, he stared at Antoine, waiting for his brother to notice him.

Antoine first went to the service window of the glass partition to give the chef the order he had just taken. When he turned around and saw his brother, he frowned and then went up to him.

"Hello, Bernard. Did Nicole finally manage to contact you?"

"I just got off the plane. She was waiting for me at the airport and had time to tell me what happened."

His breath smelled of liquor. He could not be called a drunkard, but every day he drank his few glasses of whiskey, like most Parisians who live a certain kind of life and frequent fashionable bars.

In his good periods, when things were bright, he kept to his ration, but when trouble began, he drank more.

His features then became blurred, his flesh grew flabby, and his eyes watered. That was his way of bucking himself up, of giving himself confidence. At bottom, he was weak, and it was too easy to blame the war for his shortcomings.

Antoine looked at him with a feeling of uneasiness. It was the wrong moment. A batch of customers entered, and they hesitated about choosing a free table. Antoine signaled to Joseph with a glance that he was to take over.

"Come . . ."

He led Bernard to the small door that opened on the corridor and the stairway. Bernard did not greet Fernande as he went by, which was a bad sign.

He was the only stout one in the family. He had been quite plump even as a child, and the others had made fun of his big behind. His mouth was as fleshy as a woman's, and he was almost chinless. In fact, when he was about twenty, he wore a beard for several months to hide the defect.

"Do you want to see him?"

Bernard did not answer. He could not refuse to see his father, but Antoine could feel that he had not come for that. Still wearing his overcoat, he stood for a moment in sullen silence at the foot of the bed.

"Has Mama noticed anything?"

"No. She's still the same."

"I want to talk to you."

Antoine preferred that their conversation take place elsewhere than in the first-floor living room, between the bedroom where their father was lying and the one where their mother was dozing.

"Come upstairs."

No sooner did they get to the second floor than Bernard became aggressive. He had started preparing for the meeting not only when he reached the airport but immediately after the telephone call he had received from Nicole on the Riviera.

"Has the money been found?"

"Take off your coat. Sit down."

"I asked you a question."

"Nothing has been found yet, but we haven't had much time to look. You'll admit that it's not the right moment to search every corner of our parents' apartment."

"That's too easy an answer!" sneered Bernard, who nevertheless took off his coat.

"What do you mean?"

"In the twenty years since you've been back home, Ferdinand and I have hardly ever been here. You lived here with our father. You were together from morning to night.

You knew his ways and habits. I hope you don't mind if I find it odd that you don't know what he did with his money."

"You know what he was like."

"I beg your pardon! I knew him the way a child knows its parents. I rang up Ferdinand. He'd just got home. I got the impression that he has the same doubts as I."

He lit a cigarette, looked around for an ashtray, and also looked, so it seemed, for something to drink. His hands were trembling.

"Admit that it's convenient. Papa suddenly dies when Fernande and you are alone in the house."

Antoine corrected him gently. "It happened in front of more than thirty people. And Madame Ledru hasn't left the apartment since."

"Who hired her?"

"I did."

"You see! You wait two hours to phone Ferdinand and to try to contact me."

"I couldn't leave the restaurant."

"Couldn't Joseph replace you?"

"It was hard that evening. I had important customers."

"The fact remains that when Ferdinand arrived, our father was already in a shroud, with a candle at each side."

The liquor he had drunk was beginning to have its effect. Antoine felt that his brother was wavering, that he was trying hard to continue his offensive. Without saying a word, Antoine went to get a bottle of whiskey from a small piece of furniture full of bottles. He put a glass and a jug of water on a small table.

"Aren't you having any?"

"Never during working hours. You know that."

74

Bernard had reached the point where he was mistrustful of everything. Nevertheless, he poured himself a glass of liquor and took a big swallow without water.

"I hardly got a wink of sleep last night. Some people with whom I'm doing business kept me at the casino. Did you look again this morning?"

"I haven't had time. I had to attend to the restaurant, and then the funeral. Fernande addressed the announcements."

"Is it on Tuesday?"

"I asked Ferdinand what he thought. A date had to be set. It was urgent. He preferred that it be at nine in the morning."

"Who's attending to the inheritance?"

"What do you mean?"

"It seems there's a million involved, to say nothing of the business. There are three of us. Matters like that aren't to be treated lightly. Usually a notary takes care of the interests of each party and sees to it that everything goes off properly."

"I don't know whether Father had a notary."

"Do you find it normal that he didn't draw up a will?"

"He didn't expect to come down suddenly with a stroke. Besides, people like him seldom leave a will. He must have imagined that his three sons . . ."

He bit his tongue.

"Continue," said Bernard challengingly.

"I too expected you to trust me."

"Well, I'll be damned! Papa dies, and there's no trace of the million he made over the last twenty years. *Your* million in a safe place. His has evaporated, as if by a miracle."

He stamped out his half-smoked cigarette on the carpet, though an ashtray was within arm's reach.

"It's less than twenty-four hours since Father died," explained Antoine patiently. "I found time this morning to go looking for a man named Jason on Rue Coquillière. Papa had dealings with him. I found an old building full of more or less shady-looking offices with enameled plaques on all the doors. Jason moved out three years ago. He didn't leave an address, though he told the concierge that he was retiring to a place near Villeneuve-Saint-Georges, where he had a little house."

Antoine was unable to resent his brother's behavior, and as he watched Bernard, who had stiffened in his aggressive attitude, he felt that he was making a discovery. Bernard was ageless, or rather he was every age at once. His irresolute face revealed the child of long ago, the young man who was at ease nowhere, the maturing man who had not managed to find his place in the world.

Would he grow old? Was his health good enough for that? If so, he would be one of those old men who have learned nothing and continue to talk about their dreams as if they were realities.

Hadn't there been something childish about their father too, to the very end? At the moment of his collapse, he was showing a young couple a picture of what he had been, a picture of a young man with a bristling mustache, standing on the threshold of his domain, flexing his muscles and full of self-assurance.

"When will Ferdinand be here again?"

"What do you mean?"

"I suppose the three of us are going to get together . . . We don't even know when he's going to be put into the coffin. One would think he was no one else's father but yours."

Antoine could feel that his attitude and tone and the look

on his face were expressions, not of a momentary bitterness, but of a hatred that had matured over the years.

There was a difference of nearly four years between them. Ferdinand and Antoine had been real brothers for a certain time. But Bernard had never played with the others, had never confided in them.

He would use the slightest pretext to complain about them to their mother, who defended him.

"Both of you, let your little brother alone. Aren't you ashamed to pick on him?"

The little brother! That was what he had always been. And what he still was. He was as capable now of bursting into a fit of rage and of stamping his feet and crying as when he had been a child.

"I'm warning you, Antoine, that I won't let myself be bamboozled. I have friends who are lawyers. I'm going to consult them this very afternoon. As for Nicole, when she comes here again, I'd like her to be treated like a member of the family and not like an undesirable stranger. If you must know, I've decided to marry her."

"Do you have anything else to say to me?"

"I advise you to find the will and the money. It's advisable that you do. Do you know the legal term that might be applied to your case before long? Captation of inheritance. I may seem like a nobody, but I know a thing or two about law."

He looked at the bottle hesitantly, then poured himself another drink and gulped it down.

"Don't think I'm drunk. I'm perfectly aware of what I'm saying and doing, and I'm telling you now that Ferdinand'll side with me."

He had some trouble finding the sleeves of his coat, and he put on his hat as he walked to the stairs.

"A word to the wise!"

It was grotesque, theatrical. Antoine was nonetheless overwhelmed, and he almost took a drink to buck himself up before going downstairs.

But he didn't. He waited long enough for Bernard to leave the building and then slowly returned to the Senate. Fernande glanced at him anxiously. To reassure her, he simply shrugged his shoulders before going to shake hands with an old customer.

The restaurant business was really odd! They were like actors on a stage. For hours every day his wife and he could exchange only hurried glances, at times a few words in a whisper. He had to smile, to listen to funny stories or to confidences.

At the age of forty-nine, he was beginning to walk like old Joseph. Most waiters and restaurant owners end up with flat feet. The world around them is no longer the world that others see, but numbered tables, familiar or unfamiliar faces, menus, dishes, checks.

For twenty years he had been serving the same delicacies in the same order on the same trolley. The gesture with which he offered the menu never varied, nor did the one with which he poured solemnly the first drops of Gamay d'Auvergne, Chanturgues, White Rosé of Corent or of Sauvagnat. The customer would examine the liquid as if he were a connoisseur, would smack his lips and glance at him as if they were both in on a secret.

Auguste had a brother, three years older than he, who still lived in Saint-Hippolyte. Fernande had tried to reach him all day, but in vain, for the old man had always refused to have a telephone installed.

As for his two or three children, one of whom was a girl whom Antoine remembered vaguely, he had no idea of what had become of them.

Fernande had sent a telegram. The brother's name was Hector. Antoine had been a child the last time he had seen him. He had been struck by the resemblance to his father, although his uncle's features were more weather-beaten and his skin was the color of baked clay.

There was also a Bourdin, a sister of his mother whom they had not been able to inform. She had married a Riom grocer, who was probably dead as his name was no longer in the telephone book.

While brooding over these wisps of thought, which he was unable to get out of his mind, Antoine went back and forth from the tables to the service window, sometimes going into the kitchen to explain to the chef the particular wishes of a customer.

"Above all, no garlic. No onions either."

He would sometimes look into the first room, as if expecting to see his father offer a drink on the house.

Then he would again see him lying stretched out upstairs, with his hands together, and he was unable to convince himself that his father was really and truly dead, that his mind was no longer working behind his icy forehead.

A little while before, when he had entered the bedroom with Bernard, he had felt like apologizing, like mumbling, "Excuse me, Papa."

In his mind's eye he saw them all again, Ferdinand, Véronique, Nicole, Bernard, each going up to the foot of the bed and standing motionless for a moment, as in church. The dead man lay there like an object, and they did not seem surprised to see him suddenly inert.

Antoine himself expected his father to start talking. He almost felt like saying to him, "Do you see the situation they're putting me in? I don't hold it against them, but I'd really like to avoid all this mess."

He, too, was surprised. He knew that when it came to money his father had always been reticent, mysterious, in the manner of peasants. The old man had never got used to the fact that the government assumed it had the right to ask him what he earned.

It was the fruit of his labor, of his, the labor of Auguste, who had begun to earn his living at an age when others were still playing marbles. The idea of a vacation had never occurred to him. At most, he had gone back to his home town once in a blue moon, and for years he had not even done that.

The last time he returned to Paris, he was gloomy. Shaking his head, he said, "They're almost all dead, or they'll be dead before long. It's now full of strangers, both in Riom and Saint-Hippolyte."

To him, a stranger was someone who was not from his village, from his street.

"In Riom they have stores just like those in Paris, and the women show their knees when they walk in the street."

He and Chaussard, the old butcher next door, could talk for hours on end about people who no longer existed, except in their memories and in family albums. At times, one would have thought they were sitting on a bench in school.

"Alfred, do you remember when I told him . . ."

"No, no, Auguste, it wasn't you who told him to go to hell.

It was little Arthur, whose father was a blacksmith . . . Wait, his name's on the tip of my tongue . . . He was an awful pest."

Come to think of it, didn't the two men talk about other personal matters? Both of them had succeeded in business. Chaussard, with his four butcher shops in Paris, was the richer of the two.

Hadn't they been tempted at times to compare their success? Antoine made up his mind to question old Alfred, who would be wary, for he had a tendency, like Auguste, to trust the younger generation only so far and no further.

To them, Antoine was a youngster. They probably still regarded him as if he were wearing short pants.

He was in a hurry to discuss things with Fernande. They had hardly seen each other all morning, had hardly been together except when the undertaker came by.

Then his wife had come over to show him the list of people to whom she was sending announcements.

"What do I do about the Auvergnats in Paris?"

"There must be thousands of them. We can't inform everyone. Call up and ask for a list of the members of the committee."

"Do you think they'll come with their flag and band? Your father was president of the association. I remember a funeral to which some of them even came in costume."

Meanwhile, Auguste was lying upstairs motionless, with his hands crossed on his stomach and with a rosary between his fingers as in the days when he served at mass.

"I don't know whether Riom has a local newspaper. But there must be one at Clermont-Ferrand. You ought to call up and have them insert an obituary."

They would surely forget to send announcements to cousins and second cousins, who were going to be offended.

The telephone rang near the cashier's desk. Fernande answered.

"One moment."

She glanced at her husband, who came over.

"Ferdinand," she whispered.

His brother's voice was curt.

"I've just rung up Bernard . . . Hello! . . . Do you hear me?"

"Yes . . ."

"Are you in the restaurant?"

"It's mealtime, isn't it?"

"We've decided to have everyone meet tomorrow. I suppose you close on Sunday, don't you?"

"That's right."

"Which do you prefer, the morning or the afternoon?"

"It doesn't matter to me."

"I couldn't be there before eleven in the morning, because of mass, and since we have a lot to say to each other, it's better to meet early in the afternoon."

"What time?"

"Two o'clock?"

"All right."

"You still haven't found anything?"

"No."

"I've tried to calm Bernard down."

"Thank you."

"I'll probably bring Jean-Loup and my daughter. In the long run, it concerns them too."

"See you tomorrow."

He had not taken his eyes off his wife, to whom he merely

whispered, before giving the check to a table, "Tomorrow at two . . . big family meeting."

He had spent almost an hour waiting on the benches of the local municipal office and being sent from one clerk to another before getting Ernest Jason's address. As soon as lunch was over, and without waiting for all the customers to leave, he had gone to get his car on Rue des Halles and had driven to Villeneuve-Saint-Georges.

He still had to find Rue des Ajoncs, and he asked several people where it was, but none of them knew. Finally, someone directed him to an outlying neighborhood, near a spot where several railway tracks ended, and after driving in and out of streets full of little old houses and shacks, he finally saw a plaque with the name of the street he was looking for.

The street was rather short. At one time it must have bordered on the countryside, and there were still a few trees in the little gardens. The corner house was a small empty café. He went in to ask for information and ordered a glass of beer.

"Jason? . . . No, I don't know anyone by that name in the neighborhood. Are you sure he lives on Rue des Ajoncs? You know, we've been here only two years."

She was wearing red slippers and a knitted garment that hung down over her hips. A cat was lying on a cane-bottomed chair near the cylindrical stove, the pipe of which went up to the ceiling.

The place did not look like a real café, and Antoine wondered who could be tempted to sit down in it.

A round-shouldered man holding a pair of pincers came in from the garden.

"Joseph, do you know anyone named Jason?"

"It's higher up, on the left side. He's not there any more. In fact, I think he died, but his daughter still lives in the house. It's called 'The Linnets.'"

The street seemed to have been forgotten by the expanding city. Grass was growing between the paving stones. The houses, with their wooden balconies and ill-proportioned roofs, were much alike. The only real difference was the color of the shutters. Those of the Linnets were yellow and had not been repainted for years.

The gate, which was also yellow, stood between two hedges. He opened it and crossed a small, weedy garden. When he reached the door, he rang the bell.

Nothing was stirring in the street. Nothing stirred in the house either. All he heard was trains coming and going and freight cars hitting against each other in the siding. Then a big plane turned in the bright blue sky before heading for the airport.

He rang again, then knocked at the door. Stepping back, he glanced at the windows. On the left side, he saw a face behind the net curtains.

Whereupon he knocked at the window, and the woman decided to go to the door, which she opened slightly.

"What do you want?"

He hardly saw anything of her, just about half of her head, a single eye, uncombed hair, and a dirty apron.

"Monsieur Ernest Jason lives here, doesn't he?"

"Do you know him?"

"No, I don't."

"Then what does it matter to you whether he lives here or not?"

She was crabbed. Crabbed and stupid. Needlessly aggressive. There was a mistrustful look in the one eye which he saw.

"I have an important question to ask him."

"What question?"

"It's a personal matter. At least tell me when he'll be in."

"He won't be in. He died."

"How long ago?"

"Is it any business of yours?"

"I wouldn't have asked otherwise."

"It'll be six months next week."

"Did you know him well? Was it from him that you rented the house?"

"I didn't have to rent it from him. He was my father."

He had put his foot against the door to prevent her from slamming it in his face, and he pressed slowly.

"Could I have a talk with you?"

He now saw all of her. She was fat, sick-looking, with swollen legs and a big, unhealthily pink face in which blue eyes expressed instinctive fear.

She resigned herself to letting him come in. The entrance was tiled with little squares of all colors. The room on the left was a combination living and dining room, but a dining room in which nobody ate, except a canary which was hopping about in a cage. Everything was congealed, was outside of time, like the clock, which probably had not worked for years.

"People are constantly coming to plague me," she said warily. "I can't tell them anything because I knew nothing about his business."

"Did your father live here?"

"Don't you know?"

There was something disquieting about the conversation,

about the atmosphere of the house, about the woman's attitude and expression.

"Don't I know what?"

"He died at Fresnes."

"In the prison?"

"Yes. They gave him a two-year sentence, and he died in the infirmary three months later. He'd said as much in court. He swore to them that he was innocent and that they were committing murder."

It was more and more difficult to ask questions.

"On what grounds was your father sentenced?"

"Fraud, according to them."

"What exactly was his profession? He had an office in Paris, didn't he?"

"Yes. He was an educated and intelligent man. He'd been a business agent. You haven't come to ask me for money?"

"No."

"Lots of them take advantage, because they read in the papers that my father was sentenced. So they ring the bell, and they claim they entrusted my father with their savings. So they tell me, but I knew nothing about his business."

"Isn't it true?"

"I don't know . . . He helped people when he was a business agent. It was his job to attach their property or to evict them. He didn't want to continue. It's because he was too kind that they put him in jail."

She finally sat down on the edge of a chair on which there were a piece of knitting and a ball of wool with two needles stuck in it. Antoine hesitated for a moment, and then he too sat down.

"Do you know when he was sentenced?"

"On September eleventh."

"In Paris? Were you there?"

"He didn't want me to go. When I got married, he kept his room here, but most of the time he slept in a small room behind his office. He'd been a widower for ten years. My mother suffered for a long time, and I know I'll end up as she did. My husband works on the railroad."

Reassured by the visitor's attitude, she went on talking for the sake of talking.

"Two years ago, he told me . . ."

"Are you referring to your father?"

"To whom else would I be referring? He told me he was retiring, and he came to live with us. I realized at once that he was having trouble."

"Did he tell you what it was?"

"People who had a grudge against him. Because, since he was no longer a business agent . . ."

She was losing the thread of her ideas, and Antoine could see that she was trying to remember what she meant to say.

"Wait . . . Oh, yes . . . He wanted to help people. He knew the laws, you realize? The shopkeepers, the people who work around the Market, where my father had his office, don't know them. For them he was a kind of bonesetter."

One had to enter her universe, which, as a matter of fact, began to seem rather coherent.

"Take me, for example, I'm treated by a bonesetter. The doctors are unable to find out what's wrong with me. So when my sister-in-law talked to me about the healer in Lagny . . ."

She knitted her brow. Her head felt heavy, and she was overtaxing herself. It was all too complicated for her.

"You were saying that he helped them."

"Yes . . . With all the papers one has to fill out nowadays. People don't even understand what's being asked of them. It's like with Social Security. There are questions in small print and you have to write the answer in a box or on a dotted line. So, if you make a mistake, there's trouble, and someone comes to attach your belongings."

"I understand."

"In the banks, they take your money, make you sign papers, and give you a bankbook. It's your hard luck if they attach you too. They claim there's nothing left in your account. But what's there to prove they haven't made a mistake, with the thousands and thousands of accounts they have?"

It was almost the way old Auguste would have spoken. He belonged to a time when there weren't banks on every street corner, when identity cards didn't exist, nor passports either, and when two envelopes were enough to prove who you were.

"Who took action against him?"

"I don't know. There were several of them. First there was one, then others, then still others. The one I heard about most was a locksmith named Bougerol who came here several times to raise a row. I didn't see him because my father locked me up in the kitchen, but I heard his voice and the insulting things he said. He once threatened my father that he'd settle his hash."

"Did your father ever talk to you about Auguste?"

"Auguste who?"

"Mature . . . a friend of his."

"In the end, he no longer had any friends. They all turned against him when they realized there was no hope for him . . . Who are you?"

"Auguste's son."

"Why didn't he come himself?"

"Because he's dead."

"What exactly do you want?"

"I'm trying to find out."

"To find out what?"

"My father's will hasn't turned up."

"Are you sure he made one? My father didn't leave any. It's true that he didn't leave any money either. Only this house, which he put in my name and my husband's."

"If he entrusted anyone with it, it was probably your father."

"Why?"

"Because he trusted him. It was your father who drew up all his papers."

"Have you come to ask me for money, you too?"

"No. But I suppose your father kept books, that he had documents in his office and that he brought them here when he came to live with you."

"He had a trunk full of papers that he put in the attic. He said they were of no interest."

"Are they still here?"

"The police came to get them. To turn them over to the judge."

"Didn't your father also have an address book?"

"He did."

"Are you the one who has it now?"

"Who, what?"

"Are you the one who has it?"

"No, the judge."

Beads of perspiration stood out on Antoine's forehead. He could think of no other questions to ask. He felt awkward. He had done his best not to alarm the poor woman, who, when she saw him stand up, was immediately frightened.

"Do you think there's a will?"

She, too, was now standing. She had asked the question in order to keep talking. Then she looked at the canary tenderly.

"Thank you very much. I apologize for having disturbed you."

"If only the others were as polite . . . Even women come knocking . . ."

When the door shut behind him, he breathed with relief. He walked to the corner, where he had left his car in front of the little café. The man who had informed him was in the process of putting wires between pegs.

"Did you find it?"

"Yes, I did, thank you."

The car was a pale gray Mercedes with a noiseless engine. His brothers resented that too. How had he been able to live all those years without realizing it?

Until the night before, his brothers had been his brothers. He did not see them often because each of them lived a different kind of life.

He was the only one who had remained at home, and no doubt that was why he had never been aware of their problems.

When Bernard turned up on Rue de la Grande-Truanderie, it was almost always because he needed money. He would rarely ask their father. After spending a few minutes with the two old people, which he did because he was unable to avoid it, he would take Antoine into a corner or else go outside with him, and they would walk for a while without speaking.

"I could have asked Ferdinand, but you know that they

have a hard time making ends meet, especially since they bought the apartment. I was supposed to get a rather big check on the fifteenth, but I learned yesterday that payment has been postponed until next month."

"How much?"

"Five thousand . . . Is that too much?"

He was very casual about it and wasted no time with thanks. To him the restaurant was a property that belonged more or less to the whole family.

If he preferred not to ask his father for money, it was because the old man regarded all figures as enormous.

As Bernard saw it, his brother had only to dip into the cashbox. Antoine was a shrewd article. He had the best of it. Did he deprive himself of anything? And didn't Fernande have a mink coat?

Ferdinand was a different case. He was no longer a Mature. When he was at the university, he had begun to look at his home as if he were a stranger. The ways of the family became more and more foreign to him.

In addition, Véronique had had a greater influence on him than he on her. When her father and mother were still alive, the couple wrote to them regularly, and her mother often went to see them in La Rochelle and then in Poitiers.

The grandchildren were members of his in-laws' family and were hardly ever seen on Rue de la Grande-Truanderie.

Now and then, Ferdinand and Véronique would come for lunch or dinner, but they came when the customers did, and so they didn't sit down with the members of the family, who ate at a marble-topped table near the bar.

"What do you suggest we have, Antoine?"

Antoine would jot down their order, pass it on to the chef, and then sit down beside them for a few minutes.

"How's Mama?"

She had been better, then worse, then a little better again, until there was no further question about her condition.

"Does Father drink much?"

"He has a little drink now and then. I keep an eye on him. One can't deprive him of his last pleasure."

It had always been hard for old Auguste to call his daughter-in-law by her first name.

"You're very pretty, Véronique . . ."

He would awkwardly bring her a flower, as if to tame her, though he knew very well that he never would.

"How are the children?"

Their names stuck in his throat, and besides, the names were a bit fancy.

Antoine, however, kept thinking of the old days when each in turn had crawled about on the floor, which was covered with sawdust at the time.

When he got back, he saw that Fernande was worried. She was staying upstairs, on the first floor, in his mother's bedroom, because she had given Madame Ledru the day off so that she could rest in her son's apartment.

"Did you learn anything?"

"I'm not sure . . . I've got to have a talk with Ferdinand."

He felt a need to exchange a few words with his father. The idea of the candles had not been his but Marinette's. He blew them out and parted the curtains of the window that looked out on the yard. However, he did not dare remove the rosary or the sprig of holly that was soaking in the holy water.

V

That evening, after closing the shutters of the restaurant, putting out the lights, checking the equipment, and putting the padlock on the trap door, Antoine did not go up to his own apartment on the second floor, but to his parents'.

Fernande, wearing a bathrobe, was in the dimly lit living room.

"Is she sleeping?"

"For the past hour. She's been quiet."

He went to the back room, where he switched on the ceiling light. He hesitated to sit up with the dead body. People still did that kind of thing in the country, though fewer and fewer did in the cities. He finally went over to his father and kissed him lightly on the forehead, saying inwardly, "Good evening, Father."

He walked to the door backwards, turned off the light, and went back to his wife.

"Go upstairs and sleep. I'll stay here with Mama."

"No, I'll stay. You can't look after her. A man can't give her the chamber pot if she needs it, or change her clothes."

The house had become so different in twenty-four hours! He finally went upstairs alone, undressed in the empty apartment, and went to bed.

On other Sundays, they slept late, and then they would dawdle about for the pleasure of having nothing to do. The closed shutters gave the restaurant a special atmosphere, and it was odd to go into the glass-enclosed kitchen around one o'clock and take from the refrigerator the meal that Julien Bernu had prepared for them the night before.

They would eat near the bar. In the afternoon, they would sometimes go to the movies or drive out into the country. Occasionally Auguste went with them.

But this Sunday was not like the others. When Antoine went down to the first floor in his bathrobe, his wife was giving the old lady her breakfast.

"Were you able to sleep?"

"Very well. She woke up only once."

They did not hear the familiar din of the Market. The street was empty, and all the shutters were closed. At nine o'clock, the undertaker's little truck stopped in front of the house, and a few passers-by lingered to watch his assistants carry in the heavy black hangings and then the empty coffin.

There was a sound of hammering. The men were transforming Madame Ledru's room into a mortuary chapel. Antoine had brought them a bottle of white wine and glasses, and they drank as they worked around the body.

Antoine and then his wife went up to dress. When they were together again on the first floor, Auguste was in his coffin, which was to remain open until the following evening.

Men and women from the neighborhood who were on their way to mass or simply out for a breath of air paused for a moment in front of the house and looked up at the windows, for everybody now knew that Auguste had died.

The doorbell rang five or six times in the course of the morning. Each time it was a delivery boy bringing flowers.

Antoine did not have lunch. He took a slice of ham from the refrigerator and ate it with a piece of bread. A little later, Fernande did the same. She was disturbed by the thought of the family meeting that was to take place.

Ferdinand and his wife had lunch together after mass and hardly said a word to each other. The night before, in bed, they had discussed for almost an hour Auguste's death and the questions it raised.

"I hope you'll stick up for your rights," Véronique had concluded. "In any case, I'll be there."

Bernard had had a bad night, and Nicole had had to take care of him, for he had kept drinking until he went to bed. In the morning, he was no better. He had a hangover. Sitting up in bed, where he had perspired a great deal, he asked for a drink to set himself up.

"Don't forget that you've got to have your wits about you this afternoon."

Nicole gave him a tiny glass of whiskey.

"I don't mind your drinking it. In an hour, you'll eat something. I'll let you have another drink before you leave, but that'll be all."

His head ached, and from time to time he had twinges that made him think his heart was going to stop beating.

"You'd better call the doctor. I don't feel well, Nicole."

"You'll feel better later."

"Do you think you ought to come with me?"

"I won't let you go alone."

They lived in a four-room apartment, above the shop of a picture framer, on Boulevard Rochechouart. They were six months behind with the rent.

She did not ask him why he had gone to Cannes. He had left without saying anything. She knew that it was enough for some vague friend to suggest in a bar at two in the morning that he come along.

Nicole had been a saleswoman in a smart shop on Rue Saint-Honoré and, after that, had worked as a model for two years. She still posed occasionally for women's magazines, though less and less often.

Marie-Laure and her friend Françoise were sleeping in their apartment on Avenue Victor Hugo after getting home at three in the morning. They had twin beds, like a husband and wife. Françoise wore severely tailored, rather masculine suits, but actually the two women were playing a kind of game, for there was nothing dubious in their relationship.

Françoise was the first one up. She went to prepare the coffee.

"What time is it?"

"Noon. Don't forget that you have to be at your grandfather's at two."

"You think it's necessary?"

"You promised your mother . . ."

They shared a car, a small, milky-white English convertible, which they took turns driving.

"May I have the car?"

"No. I need it to go to Louveciennes. I'll drop you off at the Market, and you'll join me at the Lemerciers'."

Jean-Loup, in a white smock and with a stethoscope around his neck, was slowly making his rounds in the children's wards, and a nurse, who took notes, was following him.

He had arranged with a colleague to replace him that afternoon. At one o'clock, he entered the interns' dining room.

It was at least three years since he had seen his grandparents. At home, when he was a child, his parents hardly ever spoke of the Matures. He did not quite understand why his parents insisted on his attending a meeting that didn't concern him.

He too had a car, a small, cheap one, which was all he needed. He arrived early. The shutters of the restaurant were closed. He entered the hallway of the building, knocked at a door on the right, then, getting no answer, went up to the first floor.

There he found Antoine, who had not yet put on his tie and jacket.

"Hello, Uncle Antoine."

His eyes looked larger because of his glasses, and he seemed quite lost.

"Haven't my parents arrived?"

The flowers had begun to fill the apartment with a sweet-ish smell.

"They won't be long. It's only ten to two . . . Do you want to see him?"

Jean-Loup stood in front of the corpse for a moment, as the others had done the night before. Meanwhile, Antoine, who was behind him, finished dressing.

"How's Grandmother?"

"Still the same."

"Does she suspect anything?"

She had not even noticed that Auguste no longer lay down beside her at night in the bed they had shared for fifty years.

"Where's it taking place?"

"I thought we'd be more comfortable downstairs."

In the first room or the second, whichever they preferred. Antoine and his nephew went down together.

"Would you like a drink?"

"No, thank you."

Jean-Loup was the tallest member of the family, and he stood with his body bent slightly forward. His father and mother knocked on the door near the cashier's desk and entered without waiting.

They kissed Jean-Loup.

"Are we late?"

"No. I came early."

"Have you seen him?"

"I went upstairs for a moment."

They barely greeted Antoine. The lights were on because of the shutters, and the two rooms looked unreal. The unlit kitchen behind the enormous sheet of glass gave the impression of being an aquarium.

A few moments later, Bernard and Nicole arrived. Véronique winced and pretended not to see Nicole.

"Are we late?"

Bernard was presentable. His eyelids were only slightly red, and he tried to behave properly.

"Isn't Marie-Laure coming?"

"She promised to be here."

They were all standing, not knowing where to sit.

"Has the mortuary chapel been set up?"

"This morning . . . They're coming tomorrow evening to close the coffin."

"Where's Fernande?"

"With Mama. I told Madame Ledru to take the day off. She was exhausted."

"Who sat up with Papa?"

"Nobody. Fernande slept on the couch in the living room."

A car stopped outside, a door slammed, and a voice said, "I hope it won't be too lugubrious."

A moment later, there were hesitant steps in the hallway. Antoine went to open the door.

"Hello, everybody! Why are you all standing and looking at each other?"

"We were waiting for you."

Antoine did not know how to get the meeting started. On the one hand, he was the host and it was he who was receiving them, but, on the other, they were in their father's home, and they all had the same rights.

"Where do we sit?"

Ferdinand sat down on the banquette to the left of the bar, and everyone else finally settled around two marble-topped tables. Jean-Loup, who had crossed his long legs, looked at the others, each in turn, as if they were strangers.

Their hats and coats were lying helter-skelter on another table.

Ferdinand, after clearing his throat, was the first to speak.

"Who decided about the cemetery?"

Everyone looked at Antoine.

"As I told you yesterday on the phone, I first thought that our father would have wanted to be buried in Saint-Hippolyte, near his parents' grave . . . He never talked about it . . . Almost everyone he knew there is dead."

He added hesitantly, "His real family is now in Paris. There's no room in Père-Lachaise Cemetery, except for those who have a vault. The only solution is to bury him in Ivry."

There was a silence. Perhaps they saw in their mind's eye an enormous modern cemetery, which was still too new and in which Auguste would have felt out of place.

"Do you think there'll be a lot of people?"

"There certainly will, when the funeral leaves the house. All the neighbors and local shopkeepers. I think that some distant relatives from Riom and Saint-Hippolyte are coming too."

"What have you arranged?"

"I've asked for twenty cars. There'll be a luncheon here for those who come from Auvergne."

The others neither approved nor disapproved. The matter did not interest them. They had mentioned the subject in order to warm up, so as not to tackle the real question immediately.

"Did you ask for prayers?"

"At the Church of Saint-Eustache."

Bernard was wriggling on his chair. He was ill at ease and kept looking at the bottles lined up behind the bar. Nicole, knowing what state he was in, was urging him to hold out a little while. It was better for him not to start drinking too soon lest he cause a fight. The night before, in his drunkenness, he had been bitter and violent and had threatened to take steps with his brothers. She had locked the drawer containing his revolver. Before leaving, she had opened it, just to be sure that he hadn't touched it.

Once again Ferdinand spoke up.

"You still haven't found the will?" he asked in a calm but cutting voice.

"I haven't looked. I prefer that you do it yourself. You know the apartment. You knew our father."

The silence that followed became menacing.

"Is there anything new about the money?"

They were all expecting Antoine to reply in the negative.

"There is."

Everyone sat up in his chair.

"Have you found it?"

"No."

"Explain what you mean."

Until then, everyone present had lived his life without great hopes of its ever changing. They knew, of course, that they would inherit something and that they were entitled to a greater or lesser share of the restaurant in which they had become strangers.

Ferdinand, for example, expected at most to be able to buy a new car, to pay off some of the debts with which he had been saddled since buying the new apartment, and even, perhaps, to spend a vacation in Italy with Véronique.

For Bernard, it would mean gaining a few months. Perhaps it would be the long-awaited opportunity of working out a deal that would stand up.

But everything had changed since the night before. Antoine had mentioned a magical figure, a figure that made people dream, on which the government had built its national lottery. A million!

It was not an abstract figure. It summoned up the idea of wealth, of a different kind of life, a life from which anxiety would disappear for ever. The fact that they might have to share the money hardly mattered. No one even thought about it. Nor did anyone remember that the mother was also one of the heirs, or that Auguste had had income tax to pay every year, or that there would be an inheritance tax.

"I first went to Rue Coquillière."

And turning to Jean-Loup, who was looking at him with great interest, he continued:

"When my father and I drew up an agreement about the restaurant, he asked a business counselor on Rue Coquillière to draft the text. The counselor was a man named Jason. I know that my father saw him again. Jason came here several times, though I didn't take much notice of him."

"Did you find him?" asked Bernard. Nicole laid her hand on his.

"I found a trace of him. His office no longer exists. The concierge mentioned a house that Jason had in Villeneuve-Saint-Georges. I went there. I finally managed to get his address through the district office."

"What did he say?"

"Nothing. He's dead."

One would have thought that he had purposely kept them in suspense. For a moment they had sat there breathless, with their jaws practically hanging. Now they were looking at him angrily, furiously.

"So you know nothing?"

"I haven't finished. I had a talk with his daughter, who's not in her right mind. Jason died in Fresnes Prison a few weeks after getting a two-year sentence for fraud."

Ferdinand was getting paler, and his right hand, in which he was holding his glasses, kept opening and closing nervously.

"If I understand correctly," he broke in, "you claim that Papa entrusted Jason with his money, that Jason was a swindler, and that, since he died in prison, we have no further recourse."

"I don't claim anything."

"Don't you find that explanation too easy? Papa is dead. Jason is dead. His daughter is crazy. And the money has disappeared without a trace."

Despite Nicole's making signs to him, Bernard got up and went behind the bar to pour himself a drink.

"It's a lousy trick!" he called out.

Everyone turned to him.

"The day Antoine came back home, we should have been wary. Especially since he shacked up with that woman."

All eyes now shifted to Antoine, who managed, with a very great effort, to remain in his chair. His fists were so tightly clenched that the knuckles were livid.

To everyone's surprise, it was Jean-Loup who broke the silence. He was very calm, as if he were speaking with the voice of reason.

"If I understand correctly, no paper has been found indicating what my grandfather did with his money."

The others nodded.

"Has anyone looked in his wallet?"

They sat there stupefied. No one else had thought of it. It was Madame Ledru who had undressed Auguste, and it had not occurred to anyone to ask what she had done with his clothes. What they were looking for was papers, documents, checkbooks, in any case something voluminous enough to correspond to the old man's investments over a period of twenty years or so.

Antoine stood up.

"If anyone wants to come with me, I'll go and look for it."

Jean-Loup got to his feet.

"I think it would be better if I went," he said.

Jean-Loup was so tall that at one point on the way upstairs he had to lower his head so as not to knock it against the low ceiling. There had just been talk of millions, and now they were opening an old brown door and entering an apartment of another age where he had been only two or three times when he was a child.

He caught a glimpse, at the far end of the living room, of part of the mortuary chapel. Flowers were lying at the foot of the coffin.

"Do you want to see her?"

Antoine felt strange in the presence of the young man who was already treating patients in hospitals and who was going to be a doctor.

Jean-Loup followed his uncle into the room which had been his grandparents' bedroom and which was still his grandmother's.

The old lady was sitting in her armchair, near the window, with a red blanket on her knees. Fernande, who had been sitting opposite her, stood up when her nephew entered.

"Hello, Jean-Loup."

"Hello, Aunt."

He went up to his grandmother and kissed her on the forehead, as he had done in the past. She drew back and rolled her eyes in search of someone she could ask for help.

"She doesn't recognize anyone."

"I know," he answered, looking at the old woman with a professional eye.

"Do you remember what was done with my father's things when he was undressed?"

"You know very well that I was downstairs. I didn't think of asking Madame Ledru."

"He must have been wearing his black suit."

Auguste had always dressed in black. His wife had always had a hard time getting him to buy a new suit. When Antoine opened the huge oak wardrobe, it was clear that his father had not given up his old things easily, even when they were threadbare, for about ten shapeless jackets were lined up on hangers.

In the same wardrobe there were also dresses, all of them black or purple, which Eugénie had not worn since she had been confined to the bedroom. On a shelf were her straw and felt hats and her husband's gray caps and round, black felt hat.

Everything in the wardrobe had been worn for years, had been part, as it were, of each one's personal role. Looking at the various objects, Antoine had the impression that each of them retained the odor of the owner's body.

He ran his hands over one of the jackets, felt something, put his hand into an inner pocket, and took out a grayish wallet.

He handed it to his nephew, who understood the gesture. Jean-Loup was embarrassed and mumbled very quickly, "You mustn't hold it against them."

It was a way of letting Antoine know that he was not necessarily with the others, that he did not belong to a clan.

"Is there anything else?" he asked.

In one of the pockets Antoine found a handkerchief and in another a short amber cigar holder that the old man had hardly ever used and a big peasant's knife.

Auguste had continued to use the knife to cut his food long after his arrival in Paris. When he opened it, he did so with an almost ritual gesture.

Fernande did not dare ask whether things were going all right. She contented herself with smiling vaguely at her husband before sitting down again near the invalid.

Bernard had taken advantage of their absence to help himself to a second drink. He had offered one to the others, but only Marie-Laure had accepted.

Jean-Loup handed the wallet to his father without opening it. Ferdinand began by feeling it.

"It contains something hard," he mumbled.

On both sides of it were pockets from which he removed papers. In order to get to the hard object he had to slide his hand to the very bottom, into what leather dealers call the secret pocket, the one that runs the whole length of the wallet.

He took out a flat, shiny key and showed it to the others, particularly to Antoine.

"Do you know what it's for?"

"I've never seen it. I'm sure it doesn't open any door or piece of furniture in the house."

He took it in his hand and saw a figure, 113, which was engraved on the key ring.

"It's a key to a safe-deposit box in a bank vault."

"How do you know?"

"Because I have almost the same kind for my box."

A sense of relief could be felt around the two marble-topped tables.

"We now have to find out which bank it is," murmured Ferdinand.

"That won't be hard. Father never went very far. Outside the neighborhood he felt as if he were in a foreign country."

He laid the key on the table, and they all stared at it, fascinated, for a question suddenly arose, one which had just occurred to all of them at the same time.

It was a Sunday. The banks did not open until nine o'clock the following morning. At that time, Ferdinand would be in court, Jean-Loup at the hospital, Marie-Laure in her shop, and Antoine in the restaurant.

Whom were they going to entrust with the key that probably gave access to the old man's fortune?

They looked up and glanced at each other. Perhaps they were a little ashamed of their thoughts?

"I'm against Antoine's going."

It was Bernard who had spoken. He was standing in the background, with a glass in his hand, and staring sternly at his brother as if challenging him again.

"You really don't know what there could be in the vault?"

"I've told you that Father never mentioned it to me."

Bernard attacked again.

"I demand that we all go together."

His statement revealed the ridiculousness, if not the odiousness, of the situation. They were all hypnotized by a shiny key that nobody wanted to touch but that nobody was willing to let anyone else take.

In what bank vault did the key open box 113? They might have to try six or seven before finding the right one. Could they go there in a crowd? And should Ferdinand, who had been unable to question Mauvis the day before because the lawyer had not shown up, put off the questioning a second time?

It was Marie-Laure who started the conversation going again.

"To whom do the three Utrillos belong?"

"To Father," replied Antoine.

"Is each of you going to take one?"

"I'll do what the others decide. I'm ready to buy them at a price set by an expert."

Ferdinand looked at his wife, and then at his daughter, whom he asked, "Do you have any idea what they're worth?"

"Anywhere between fifty and a hundred thousand francs apiece. It depends on when they were painted."

They belonged to the period when women wore long skirts and had big behinds.

"Why are you so eager to buy them?" asked Ferdinand, who was still mistrustful.

"So that they remain where they've been for such a long time. They used to be in the bedroom upstairs. When I first saw them, as when you did, they were in the back room . . . You really won't have anything to drink? Fernande apologizes for not being here, but she has to stay with Mama. If you leave her alone for a moment, she imagines she's been abandoned."

It was not an ordinary family meeting. There should have been coffee cups or wine glasses on the tables. There should also have been a relaxed atmosphere.

It was as if each of them were trying to find something to say to break the silence, especially Ferdinand, who liked playing the role of eldest brother and who, as such, was supposed to be acting as chairman.

"The most urgent thing is obviously to find the bank."

They were going around in a vicious circle. What was to be done with the key until then?

Again it was Jean-Loup who found the solution.

"All you have to do is put it in an envelope and seal it. The three brothers can initial the seals."

"I wonder whether there's any wax in the house. I saw a piece not long ago in one of the drawers in my bedroom."

As Antoine closed the door behind him, Bernard growled, "*He's* not worried. He already has his share."

Although Nicole looked at him beggingly, he went behind the counter again to fill his glass. Marie-Laure eased his conscience by calling out to him, "May I have one too, Uncle Bernard?"

Her mother looked at her in amazement.

"Have you started drinking whiskey?"

"I've been drinking it for a long time, you know. Even when I was still living at home. Only I didn't dare do it in front of you. Would you like a drink, Papa? You don't mind a shot of whiskey from time to time either."

"Whiskey for everybody?"

With Antoine out of sight, they relaxed, as if on vacation.

"Not for me," snapped Véronique.

Bernard, delighted with his role, was filling the glasses.

"Ice?"

"Just plain water."

Antoine stayed away for quite a while. He gave himself time enough to exchange a few words with Fernande.

"How's it going?"

"Better than at the beginning, thanks to Jean-Loup."

"What are you going to do with that candle and the wax?"

"We found a key to a vault in Father's wallet. Nobody wants to trust anyone else with it. We're going to seal it."

He had also found a brown envelope. When he returned to the restaurant, he looked at the glasses on the table without saying a word, lit the candle, and handed the wax and the envelope to his brother.

"You're used to this kind of thing, Ferdinand."

The judge felt a little ashamed. In the grayness of his office or in the course of visits to the scene of a crime, he had often had to deal with sordid affairs. And now he and his family were involved.

He put the key into the envelope, pasted down the flap, and melted the wax.

"What are we going to sign with?"

As if ironically, though unintentionally so, Antoine handed

him a silver toothpick. Each of the brothers then initialed the five wax seals with it.

"What do we do with it now?"

"I suggest . . ."

Antoine and Bernard, who had spoken at the same time, stopped at the same time.

"Say it."

"I suggest that Ferdinand keep the envelope."

"That's exactly what I was going to say."

"For once we agree."

As if to celebrate the easing of the tension, Antoine went to the bar to get the bottle and a glass, poured himself a few drops, and put the bottle on the table.

"Help yourselves."

Jean-Loup, who was sitting with his legs crossed, was watching the scene as if he were a stranger. The death of Auguste was forcing him to examine the family background, and he was observing things coolly and objectively. Perhaps he was more aware than his father of the distance between Ferdinand and himself.

In the apartment, too, he was less at ease than in his pigeonhole at the hospital. And when he looked at his sister from time to time, he felt no emotional tie.

"I think you're losing sight of an important point," he finally declared in a neutral tone.

Everybody turned to him.

"Uncle Antoine spoke to us earlier about a certain Jason who was sentenced a few months ago to two years in prison for fraud."

He turned to his father.

"It ought to be easy for you to find out which examining magistrate handled the affair."

"That's no problem, because each of us more or less specializes. Probably Pénaillon or Mourine. They deal with such matters by the dozen."

"Are you friendly with them?"

"I know them. We shake hands when we meet in the corridor."

"I wonder whether, among the papers that were found at Villeneuve-Saint-Georges, of which there seems to have been a trunkful, he found any concerning my grandfather."

The finding of the key had made them forget the shady counselor and had restored their optimism.

"What else is there in the wallet?"

The question was addressed to Ferdinand, and it was with great reluctance that he searched in his father's wallet. He first pulled out an identity card that had been renewed ten years before and a prescription for glasses signed by an eye doctor on Rue du Temple.

"Did Father wear glasses?"

Antoine was the most surprised of all.

"I never saw him with them."

"Do you know about such things?" asked Ferdinand, handing the paper to his son.

"Not much. It's for reading glasses, rather strong ones, it seems to me."

The prescription, which was three years old, illustrated the old man's secrecy or sense of shame. His eyes had been getting weaker. He had had difficulty reading the newspaper. He had no doubt waited a long time before consulting an eye doctor in the neighborhood.

The prescription reminded Antoine of what his father had been doing a few minutes before he collapsed. The old man was proudly showing a young couple a photograph of himself standing in front of his restaurant in 1920, when he was in the prime of life. He had continued to hold himself erect and to throw out his chest. He was proud of his vitality and laughed at Dr. Patin, who prescribed medicines for him.

He had never ordered the glasses, but he had nevertheless kept the prescription in the event that they became absolutely necessary.

"Who is it?" asked Marie-Laure, who was leaning over her father.

He had taken from the wallet a faded photo with broken corners in which a two- or three-year-old boy was looking straight ahead as if he were very sure of himself and were defying the future.

"It's me. I didn't remember the picture."

"I wasn't born yet," said Antoine.

Ferdinand had been an only child at the time. Auguste had a bluish-black mustache that he set every night with a transparent gadget. His wife did the cooking for twenty-five or thirty people, and the menu was written in chalk on a slate.

There was also a photograph of Bernard on the day of his first communion and one of Antoine as a soldier.

They were all surprised. It had never occurred to them that Auguste might be sentimental, and yet he had kept the photos of his three sons in his old wallet.

The last photo, which was tiny and crackled, was protected by a plastic case. It had been cut out of a group picture, and if they had not found it in their father's wallet, the sons would never have recognized it.

It was their mother when she was very young, perhaps sixteen. She was wearing two braids, and the hair over her forehead was tousled. The collar of her dark dress, which covered her neck, had a lace collaret.

They found nothing else, except a copy of a birth certificate, also yellowed and crackled, which dated from the time of Auguste's arrival in Paris. Was it a precautionary measure that his parents had taken, at a time when identity cards did not exist, in the event that he got lost or was injured in an accident?

"Ferdinand . . ."

Véronique was showing him her wrist watch.

"Keep the wallet until we meet again so that we can each choose a few souvenirs."

"Don't forget the envelope," said Bernard.

Ferdinand put it gravely into his pocket and stood up.

"If Antoine has time tomorrow to go to the banks in the neighborhood, which he knows better than we do, he might ask whether Father had an account or a vault in one of them. Will you have time, Antoine?"

"I may. I expect that as soon as people receive the announcement, they'll start dropping in."

"Aren't you closing the restaurant?"

"It's not the custom to. Only on Tuesday."

"If anything turns up, call me in court. Bernard, will you be at home?"

He would be there, in bed. Nicole foresaw it, for she had been unable to keep him from drinking, and he had reached the point where he was going to continue.

The meeting was ending better than it had begun. They looked at each other without quite knowing how to break up.

Ferdinand was putting on his gray topcoat, Nicole her leopard-skin coat, and Bernard his camel's-hair, though he was having trouble finding the armholes.

Jean-Loup, who was coatless, was the only one who shook hands with Antoine.

"See you Tuesday," he said.

They all walked to the hallway, where they passed two children from the third floor who were dressed up in their Sunday best. They were followed by their parents.

"Pierre and Lina, let the people go by."

And the parents nodded respectfully.

VI

Véronique, who was in her bathrobe, had just finished putting her hair up in curlers. She called out from the bathroom, "Aren't you undressing?"

It was ten in the evening. Ferdinand, who had not taken off his gray suit, which was a kind of uniform for him, was in the living room. He was reading a magazine article, though his mind was elsewhere.

Upon leaving Antoine's place—the others were already saying and thinking "Antoine's place" and not "Father's place"—Jean-Loup had rushed off to the hospital and Marie-Laure had asked her parents, "Could you drive me to Louveciennes?"

During the drive, they had been silent and preoccupied almost all the time, as if they all had a guilty conscience. About twenty cars, including two Rolls-Royces and a number of very smart sports cars, were parked in front of the villa to which the daughter was going.

"Whose house is it?"

"A fellow who runs a big advertising firm."

Ferdinand and his wife had had dinner in a small restaurant in Versailles before going home, where they did not know what to do and where there was no television program that interested them. Véronique had filed her nails. Her husband had read. They had fallen into the habit, without any particular reason, of going to bed earlier on Sunday than on other days. Besides, Ferdinand went to bed earlier and earlier, perhaps because he and his wife had nothing to say to each other.

The doorbell rang, and they both started.

"Do you mind going?"

He stood up, feeling intrigued and at the same time vaguely uneasy. Nobody ever rang their bell so late. When he opened the door, he saw Bernard, who was very excited, and Nicole, who was resigned and watchful.

"Excuse me, Ferdinand . . . I can imagine what you're probably thinking, and I admit straight off that you're right: I'm drunk."

He staggered toward the living room and let his coat fall on the carpet without bothering to pick it up.

"Isn't your wife here? Véronique's a swell gal, and I'd like her to know that I think so."

Nicole had been driving ever since they had left the restaurant. She knew that there was no point in going home. It was too late. Bernard had got under way. All she could do was hope for the best.

"One more, just one, Nicole. I absolutely must find that guy. I've forgotten his name. It's not because I'm drunk. There are people like that, I can't manage to remember their names."

"What does he do?"

"He's a lawyer. He's always being mentioned in the papers. We had a drink together a week ago. No, it was two weeks ago. It doesn't matter. Anyway, it's absolutely essential that I talk to him, you realize, because I'm the only one who smelled a rat, though I didn't let on . . . Ferdinand's a judge, eh? Well, Ferdinand's a half-wit, he didn't understand a thing, or else he's in on it and if so he's a son of a bitch."

They had wandered from bar to bar. She had signaled to the successive bartenders, who knew her, to pour as little whiskey as possible into their glasses. He had refused to have dinner and contented himself with nibbling peanuts.

He had finally found the man he was looking for, who really was a lawyer. The man was in a not much better state than he. Bernard had then prevailed upon Nicole to drive him to his brother's place.

"Is it any of my business or not? Am I a Mature or not, eh?"

Véronique, who was anxious, emerged from the bathroom with a towel tied around her head to hide the curlers.

"Don't be afraid, Véronique . . . I know you're ashamed of Nicole because we live in sin. I swear to you that we'll be married in a month, and, if you really want us to, we'll even have a church wedding . . . I was saying to my brother that you're a swell gal. Nicole thinks so too. She's furious because I've had one too many and because I'm disturbing you, but it was ab-so-lute-ly necessary."

He was rarely in such a state. Oddly enough, he seemed younger when he let himself go. One had the feeling that he was defenseless. He gave the impression of wanting to be taken for a man at any cost.

"In the first place," he began, with a broad gesture, "everything we said this afternoon is a lot of crap."

He turned to Ferdinand with a look of distrust.

"Am I right, yes or no?"

"I don't know what you mean."

"The key, for example, that was a lot of crap, right?"

"Sit down."

He dropped into a chair, which he had not realized was so low, and for a moment he was surprised.

"Neither you nor I nor Antoine nor anyone has the right to go and open the vault, even with the key . . . What do you have to say?"

"It's true that there are a certain number of formalities."

"Formalities my eye!"

He was proud of himself. It was he, the youngest, the one who was regarded as a poor slob, who had discovered the truth of the matter.

Despite the fact that Ferdinand was a judge, he had let himself be taken, unless it was he who had taken them all.

"What does it say, Article . . . Article what, Nicole?"

"Which one?"

"The first one I asked you to write down."

She took from her bag a red date book in which she had taken notes so as not to irritate him.

"774 . . ."

"Good! Do you have a statute book, Ferdinand?"

He was triumphing.

"I know the article you refer to."

"Go get your statute book."

His brother came back with the book.

"*An estate may be accepted unreservedly or without liability to debts beyond its assets.*"

"Well and good! And who has the right to accept it only without liability to debts beyond its assets? Ha! Ha! Ha! Any one of the heirs . . . you get me? . . . Véronique, if you want to be an angel, let me have something to drink."

She looked at Nicole, who shrugged.

"Don't be afraid . . . I know how to behave, and I won't soil your carpet."

He laughed. He was master of the situation.

"I'm clearheaded, you understand? I'm drunk but clearheaded."

He repeated the last word three or four times with great delight.

"It's because I'm clearheaded that I understood . . . My friend . . . what's his name, Nicole?"

"Liotard."

"Liotard . . . a great lawyer . . . . Do you know Liotard, Ferdinand?"

"I've heard of him."

"We had a drink together, and I told him what was bothering me, because he's like a brother . . . Excuse me! Not a real brother like you, you understood what I mean . . . Now look at the article whose number Nicole is going to give you."

"Article 793."

Ferdinand read it in order to keep him quiet:

"The statement by an heir that he wishes to be considered as such only without liability to debts beyond its assets must be filed in the record office of the county court which . . ."

"Fine! The county court . . . Do you see what I'm getting at? In the next article the statute states that the declaration is followed by a faithful and exact inventory of the estate . . . Am I clearheaded or not? . . . Thanks, Véronique . . . Here's to everyone's health . . . To the health of our poor father . . . They have three months in which to start the inventory, which may go on for a long time . . . What's the upshot? . . . That Antoine can string us along as long as he likes and during that time can monkey with the accounts."

His mind dashed off in another direction.

"You see, Ferdinand, Antoine and we two aren't on an equal footing. You and I are poor suckers . . . Yes we are! Yes we are! . . . I know what I'm saying . . . You mustn't be ashamed of it . . . Rascals are never poor suckers . . . You may be a judge, but you earn hardly enough to live on, and me, I've never had any luck . . . I'm just as intelligent as Antoine . . . even more . . . only, I . . ."

Words failed him. He took a swallow and frowned. His face was all red. He was pathetic. He looked at his brother with his big moist eyes.

"Nicole, what's his name again?"

"Liotard."

"Right . . . Do you know him?"

"I've already told you."

"I beg your pardon . . . He gave me his legal opinion at Jean's, a bar where you can find him almost any evening . . . Have you ever been to Jean's?"

"No."

Never mind! He dropped the matter. He was searching his memory, anxious not to lose the thread. It was very hard, all the more so because he realized the importance of what he had to say.

"You were about to go to bed . . . I beg your pardon, Véronique . . . Only, tomorrow . . . To begin with . . ."

To begin with what? In the car, he had planned what he was going to say. Standing at Jean's mahogany bar, Liotard had delivered a lecture on the laws governing inheritance. He knew the articles in the statute book by heart and reeled them off, giving the exact number of each and every one, like a juggler tossing balls into the air.

"I need money. I'm not trying to hide the fact, and I'm not ashamed of it . . . Honest people spend their time running after money . . . You need money too, Ferdinand. I dare you to say you don't."

It was better to agree with him in order to avoid an outburst, for in that state he was capable of losing his temper, of stamping like a child, of saying what he thought about everyone. Nicole, who realized the danger, looked at Ferdinand and his wife beggingly, as if pleading with them to be patient.

"All right! What was I saying?"

"That we needed money."

"Now supposing Antoine accepts the inheritance only without . . . how does it go?"

"Without liability to debts . . ."

"That gimmick allows him to string us along for months, for years . . . That's not all . . . There's another article about joint . . . joint . . ."

"Joint property . . ."

"If he wants to, Antoine has the right to run the restaurant without selling it and without giving us anything. Is that fair?"

"Not completely . . . more or less . . ."

"Well? . . . Are you beginning to understand? . . . Who has the upper hand? . . . Did our father ever keep books? Did he know anything about bookkeeping? Who's been attending to money matters for the last twenty years? . . . We found a key, well and good . . . But we don't have the right to use it before everyone agrees to accept the inheritance without further discussion . . . Without liability to debts. You get it?"

No. Ferdinand did not see what his brother was driving at.

"Either we accept and we get the money right away or we accept only without liability to debts and we can wait for years, until the restaurant's not worth a damn . . . What was it that Antoine said? . . . That it would probably be demolished in three years . . . You know what Liotard . . ."

He smiled, proud of having thought of the lawyer's name all by himself.

"You know what Liotard called our affair? A hornet's nest . . . Without an inventory, Antoine tells us what he wants and gives us whatever figures happen to suit him . . . With an inventory, he has all the time in the world . . . Correct?"

It was correct. Ferdinand, who had thought about the matter, had deliberately avoided raising the question that afternoon. Two days earlier, he had not been expecting that there would be any change in his material situation, but ever since there had been talk of millions, he had been as impatient as Bernard and was making an effort to avoid complications.

He wasn't proud of himself. He kept telling himself that he was acting the way he was for Véronique's sake, so that she would have a better life.

He, too, was jealous of Antoine, who had just proved to be the rich member of the family. He was the least educated of the three, most probably the least intelligent. Fernande had been a streetwalker, and yet the two of them were a real couple. There was a deep understanding between them.

"Let me have another drink, Véronique. I swear it'll be the last. Don't worry, Nicole. As soon as I finish what I have to say, we'll go. Tomorrow I'll be sick, yes, I know . . . I apologize . . . You'll have to take care of me . . . Ferdinand, don't you ever drink?"

"Very seldom."

"You're lucky. When I get going, I make Nicole unhappy and I get sore at myself. You don't know Nicole. She's the one who refused to get married, because she was afraid it would damage my reputation . . . I did my best to explain to her that . . ."

He stood up and, at the last second, avoided falling headfirst onto the little table where he had put his glass. Regaining his balance, he went over to the young woman and kissed her hand.

"To begin with, all three of us are Father's sons, right? And the three photos were in his wallet, right or wrong? That's proof, and Antoine can say what he likes . . . If you and I can't come to an agreement, Antoine'll trick us . . . There's something else the lawyer said to me . . . Liotard . . . You see that I remember everything, that I'm clearheaded . . . It's about our mother . . . Under what system were they married?"

"Joint estate . . ."

"Consequently, she's entitled to half . . . If we go to the conciliation magistrate, she'll have to come along or she'll have to sign papers . . ."

Véronique was looking at her husband in amazement, even with reproach in her eyes. Why hadn't he spoken to her about these possible complications?

"Could *you* drag Mama to the judge's office?"

"No."

"Do you think she's still capable of signing her name? Someone has to hold her hand . . . Dr. Patin knows very well that she's no longer in her right mind. In which case, as Liotard says, a guardian or family council has to be appointed."

Again he was deep in his chair, with his head down. He kept running his hand over his forehead.

"We'll be taken, Ferdinand . . . That's why I came . . . That's why I disturbed you . . . We mustn't be taken . . . We've been taken all our life . . . You know me . . . I'm a good guy . . . I trust people . . . It's because I trust them . . . I've drunk too much . . . When this is all over, I'll stop drinking . . . If I drink, it's because . . . Nicole?"

"What?"

"You remember what he said at the end? . . . Excuse me . . . I'm beginning to get mixed up . . . One more drink, Véronique, a tiny little one."

"No!" exclaimed Nicole. "If you let him have it, he'll fall asleep and I won't be able to take him home."

"I'm clearheaded."

"I know."

"So, tell them . . ."

Nicole was embarrassed. She looked at them hesitantly, one after the other.

"It's no business of mine . . . I didn't even know Liotard . . . He was tight and was listening to the sound of his own voice. His advice may be worthless. According to him, you must absolutely avoid getting involved with judges and you must get as much money from Antoine as possible . . . That's exactly how he put it. As for the conciliating magistrate and permission to open the vault, he claims that it's a trivial formality and that your mother's signature is enough, even if someone has to help her write her name."

She was dizzy with confusion. It made her uncomfortable to see Véronique, who had always given her the cold shoulder, watching her with curiosity and even with budding sympathy.

"What do you think, Ferdinand?"

"I've got to think it over. I've got to reread the statute, because I've never dealt with common law and I have to refresh my memory."

"A pig in a poke!" exclaimed Bernard, who had remained silent for some moments.

Since he did not explain what he meant but just sat there sleepily with a smug smile on his face, Nicole spoke up.

"Liotard said that it amounted to buying a pig in a poke. In order to be able to open the vault, you first have to accept the inheritance. But nobody knows what the vault contains."

"We could also inherit debts," mumbled Bernard, who tried to laugh and at the same time reached for his empty glass.

Véronique started.

"He was obviously joking. I think he was teasing Bernard . . . All the same, he was bothered by the Jason matter."

"I'll look into it tomorrow morning. Even if I have to postpone my interrogation until Tuesday—no, Wednesday."

He was forgetting about his father's funeral.

"Come, Bernard . . . Now that you've said what you had to say . . . You're sleepy . . . And so are Ferdinand and Véronique."

"Do you agree, Ferdinand?"

"Of course."

Neither of them made clear what it was that they agreed to, Bernard because he was incapable of doing so and Ferdinand because he had forced himself to say "Of course" in order to get rid of his brother.

"Stand up."

She helped him get to his feet, picked up his coat from the floor, and handed it to him.

"You know, Ferdinand, it did something to me to see that photo of you when you were little. After all, we're brothers. Right? We ought to defend each other like brothers. That's what I said to Nicole, who didn't want me to come."

It took several minutes to get him to the elevator. Ferdinand and his wife leaned over the shaft and waited until they heard the front door close and the noise of a car going off.

The alarm rang at 5 A.M., as usual, and Antoine reached out in the darkness and turned it off before Fernande awoke. He groped his way through the bedroom, put the light on in the bathroom, and began to shave with the anxious look of a man who has a hard day ahead of him.

It was still dawn when he began his rounds of the vegetables, which smelled of damp earth, and then of the fish and shellfish sections.

He did not hurry. Plodding along, he shook the hands that were offered him here and there and said "Thank you" when anyone mumbled "My condolences, Antoine."

He arrived at Léon's place and for a few moments silently watched the butcher cut up and dress meat. It was Léon who spoke first.

"My father won't admit it, but he had an awful shock. Yesterday I saw him walk up and down in front of the restaurant four or five times and look up at the windows on the first floor. He and Auguste were very fond of each other. They were the last two. And now my old man is waiting for his turn."

A little later, after Antoine had given his order, Léon asked, "Can I go to see him today?"

"Of course . . . By the way, thanks for the flowers."

"That's the least I could do."

Jules had had time to open the shutters and start the coffee. There were more people than usual in the first room. People from the Market, as always at that time of day. The room smelled of spiked coffee and warm croissants. Antoine had the feeling that the people were not looking at him in quite the way they usually did. He was no longer Auguste's son. He had taken the old man's place and had become the boss.

"Jules, let me have a cup of coffee."

Jules whispered in his ear, "Some of them have asked whether they can go up and see him."

"I'll tell you when I come down."

Fernande had already thought about it. She was wearing a very simple black dress, the one she wore when she sat at the cashier's desk. She was helping Madame Ledru tidy up the apartment and install the old lady in her chair.

"I suppose they'll be coming by?"

"Yes. Some of them downstairs have already asked."

"They can come up. Liselotte will have to take my place at the desk at lunchtime. I just received a phone call from Riom, from someone named Gabriel Mature, who, if I understood correctly, is a distant cousin of yours. He's an assistant stationmaster. He said that since he doesn't have to pay his fare, he'll be glad to come to the funeral if you find a room for him in the neighborhood."

"What did you say to him?"

"That we'd find one. I'll attend to it in a little while."

He went downstairs.

"They can go up," he said to Jules.

Then he went to the kitchen to work with Julien Bernu. As Fernande was too busy in the apartment, it was he who wrote the names of the day's specials on the menus.

When he went out, flowers were being delivered. There would be other deliveries throughout the day. Because of the black hangings, they could not open the casement window in the room where the coffin was, and the smell was getting sickening. It had already begun to spread through the house.

At about nine-thirty he entered the Crédit Lyonnais, the bank on Rue Saint-Honoré where he had an account. He knew the assistant manager, Monsieur Grangier, who attended to his affairs when necessary.

"My condolences, Monsieur Mature. I heard about what happened to your father. As a matter of fact, when does the funeral start from the house?"

"Tomorrow morning, at nine."

"I'll be there, of course. Is there anything I can do for you?"

"My brothers and I are rather puzzled. My father didn't leave any papers, but we found a key in his wallet."

He took his bunch of keys from his pocket and separated the vault key from the others.

"It's about an eighth of an inch longer than this one, and

shinier. The ring is round instead of oval, and the number 113 is engraved on it."

"Do you have it with you?"

Antoine blushed before answering.

"No . . . I gave it to my elder brother."

"If it's a vault key, as I have every reason to think, it's probably from the Comptoir d'Escompte, because their keys resemble your description. Do you suppose your father banked with a neighborhood branch?"

"He seldom left the neighborhood."

"Would you like me to ring up my colleague? There's a branch on Boulevard de Sébastopol. One moment . . ."

Among the several telephones on his desk he chose the one that was an outside line. He dialed the number.

"May I please speak to Monsieur Favret . . . Tell him that Monsieur Grangier would like to speak to him . . . Have a seat, Monsieur Mature . . . Hello! . . . Favret? . . . Very well, thanks . . . Yours too? . . . Give her my regards . . . I'm calling for a bit of information . . . The father of one of our good clients has just died . . . Mature, yes . . . What? . . . That's exactly why I called you . . . His son is in my office . . . They found a key with the number 113 . . . No paper, no . . . It's in your bank? . . . One moment, I'll ask him . . . There are several heirs, aren't there? Three brothers, if I'm not mistaken . . . Is your mother still alive? . . . Favret? The mother and three sons . . . They're all over twenty-one . . . The conciliating magistrate . . . Thank you very much . . . I'll tell him . . ."

He was somewhat like a magician who had just performed a stunt.

"As you see, it wasn't complicated. It was at the Comptoir

d'Escompte on Boulevard de Sébastopol that your father had a safe-deposit box . . . On the other hand, he never opened an actual account. I suppose it was because you looked after his affairs . . . All that's necessary is that you and your brothers appear before the district magistrate on Rue du Louvre, or even, I think, his clerk."

"What about my mother?"

"Can't she go with you?"

"She no longer leaves her bedroom."

"You'll be given a form for her to sign . . . I'm delighted to have been able to help, especially since you probably have your hands full."

Antoine hardly noticed that spring was in the air, that women were wearing light-colored dresses, and that men, including himself, were not wearing coats for the first time that year.

At home, there was a continuous stream of people going up and down the old staircase, and every fifteen minutes a messenger boy arrived with flowers or a wreath.

He rang up the courthouse and had to wait quite a while before getting Ferdinand at the other end.

"This is Antoine."

"As a matter of fact, I expect to drop by in an hour. Will you be there?"

"I will . . . I found the bank."

"How did you manage?"

"I asked the assistant manager of mine. I described the key to him, and he rang up the Comptoir d'Escompte on Boulevard de Sébastopol. Papa had a box, but not an account."

"I'll be over."

Too bad for René Mauvis. He could wait till Wednesday. He was a nobody, the kind of person who was shoved about and squeezed in crowded subways at 6 p.m., and no one would ever have talked about him but for the fact that he was suspected of two murders. As for the lawyer, Ferdinand had already rung him up.

"I'm terribly sorry about upsetting your schedule. The questioning could have taken place on Saturday, and it's not my fault if I'm obliged to put it off until Wednesday . . . No! Absolutely impossible . . . Tomorrow's my father's funeral."

At the same time, Antoine was relieving Fernande for a little while so that she could go out for a breath of air. The apartment on the first floor was suffocating. There were flowers everywhere. They overflowed the mortuary chapel and invaded the living room, where the couch was covered with them.

Fernande had placed a silver tray on a small table, and on it lay about twenty calling cards, some with the corner turned down.

It was all new to Antoine. There had never been a death in the family, and he felt bewildered. He did not recognize the two undertaker's assistants who came to shut the coffin.

He stood in the living room, not far from the open door, as Fernande had done. The visitors hesitated for a moment and then went up to him and shook hands, while muttering something more or less unintelligible.

"Thank you."

He did not know all of them, for there were many who were not from the Market. Workmen who had done a job for them looked completely different because they were wearing suits, whereas Antoine had always seen them in their work clothes.

It took old Hector, Léon's father, a long time to climb the stairs, and when he arrived, the coffin was shut. He remained standing, very erect, looking at it a long time, without paying any attention to the people who came and went.

Then he dipped the sprig of holly in the holy water and solemnly made a cross in the air above his friend's body.

He would live another year or two, perhaps only until the following winter. Then it would be Antoine's turn to greet him one last time in the nearby apartment.

When Fernande returned, she whispered to him, "Your brother's upstairs. I thought it was better to have him come up because they've started to set the tables downstairs and it won't be long before the staff has lunch."

He went up to the second floor and found Ferdinand standing in the middle of the living room.

"Not too tired?" asked the judge. "I didn't expect such a crowd."

"Neither did I."

"Unfortunately, we can't help you. It's so long since I left the neighborhood that I no longer know anyone. And obviously Véronique can't help either."

"Obviously."

"I thought it would be better if you and I had a personal talk. Bernard and Nicole came to see us last evening."

Antoine looked at him, but with hardly any surprise. He felt he had no contact with reality that morning, and he caught himself wondering what his brother did at home in the evening.

There were people in the restaurant, people on the first

floor, and Ferdinand in his own apartment. And in an hour, immediately after the staff had lunch, he would have to take up his post in the Sideshow and hand the menu to his customers.

"Bernard had been drinking and was rather far gone . . . You know what he's like . . . Now that he's caught a glimpse of a fortune, he wants it right away and is scared stiff of not getting his hands on it."

"What's on his mind?"

"The opening of the safe-deposit box, naturally. But first of all, I have a question to ask you. I suppose, of course, that you're going to declare that you're an heir."

"What do you mean? Do you mean I'm not if I don't?"

"Of course you are. There are certain legal details. Now listen to me . . . I've given the matter a great deal of thought. We have two ways of settling the inheritance. Each of us can declare that he's an heir without liability to debts, in which case it's the county court that deals with the matter and that appoints the experts . . ."

Antoine, who only a few minutes before had been in the dead man's bedroom, looked at his brother and frowned.

"Is there anyone who's asking for an inventory?"

"Not I . . . Nor Bernard either . . . We both trust you, and as for Mama, poor thing, it's self-evident . . ."

Then why did Ferdinand look so embarrassed and anxious? He was rubbing and twisting his hands the way he did when he was a child and had to show his father a report card that he wasn't proud of.

"I don't see what can complicate things. My books are at your disposal. They can be examined by any accountant you like. As for the business, it's easy to tell approximately what it's worth."

133

"You're right. Or rather, you'd be right if there weren't that vault. We have no idea how much money our father left. In order to open the box, we have to get permission from the judge."

"I know."

"I called him up a little while ago . . . All three of us, the sons, will have to sign, in his presence, a statement that we accept the inheritance."

"What about Mama?"

Ferdinand avoided looking at him.

"If we admit that she's not in her right mind, there'll be complications . . . I've brought a form for her to sign."

"She's incapable of writing."

"Not if your wife holds her hand."

Antoine almost jumped to his feet with indignation.

"What's going on anyway?" he exclaimed, trying not to lose his self-control. The blood had rushed to his head, and he looked at his brother grimly.

"Nothing's going on. I'm trying to explain things as simply as possible. The law provides that, if there are no minors, the rightful heirs can divide the inheritance without formalities. I've come to ask you, in Bernard's name and my own, if that's all right with you."

"But what about Mama?"

"I don't think we're wronging anyone by helping her sign a paper of which she would approve if she were in her right mind. The vault has to be opened, right or wrong?"

"Yes, it has to be, but . . ."

Antoine was about to say, "But we might wait until Father was buried."

He was being rushed, he was being hounded. He began to

wonder why his brothers were in such a hurry and whether they were setting a trap.

"In that case, the box will be opened at two-thirty this afternoon. I've made an appointment with the judge for two o'clock. Each of us will sign the same paper that Mama signs. Here, this one's for Mama. Ask your wife to . . ."

Antoine took it from his hands and left. He was no longer red, but pale. He pushed aside, almost roughly, some strangers who were barring his way on the landing. He motioned to Fernande, who was receiving condolences, to follow him for a moment, and he took her into the mother's bedroom.

"It seems that it's necessary that she sign . . . Can you hold her hand?"

She looked at him in surprise.

"Did Ferdinand . . . ?"

He nodded.

"Mightn't we have trouble?"

"He claims we won't. If we don't have her signature, we'll have to declare that she's insane and we'll be involved in court action."

She was more wary than he.

"Antoine, have you thought it over?"

He was so disgusted that he would have done anything at that moment, would have signed anything in order to have peace.

"Do it . . . I'll take your place meanwhile."

He went into the living room and stood in the middle of the floor. His face was frozen, and he kept mumbling mechanically to those who came up to him and put out their hand, "Thank you . . . It's kind of you . . . Thank you

. . . Yes, tomorrow at nine . . . Thank you . . ."

It seemed to him an eternity before Fernande returned and slipped the paper into his hand.

"Did you do it?"

"It wasn't easy."

Then he went up to join his brother.

VII

"Did your wife manage it?"

Antoine handed him the paper without saying anything, without even having glanced at it. Ferdinand put it into his wallet, but there was no sign of his leaving.

"I've got to talk to you about this Jason . . . I'd rather that Bernard weren't present, because he'd start worrying again."

Antoine looked at him with indifference.

"It was my colleague Mourine who dealt with the affair, just as I thought. I had a short talk with him this morning. Jason was one of those shady business counselors of which there are still quite a number around Porte Saint-Martin, Porte Saint-Denis, and the Market. Some of them specialize in buying and selling businesses. Others make loans at high interest. Still others help the workmen and shopkeepers draw up their income-tax declaration and keep their account books . . . Jason did all those things. In recent years, the district attorney's office stuck its nose into his affairs two or three times, but without ever finding anything objectionable . . . His clients had confidence in him, and he acted as their accountant, notary, lawyer, and banker . . . Do you see what I mean? . . . He was what simple people, especially in the country and small towns, call a business counselor . . . People like him are wily . . . From what I gather, because it's not my field, he sometimes bought annuities . . . He also began—and even reputable notaries are sometimes tempted to do the same thing—to speculate with his clients' money . . . One fine day he found himself in a tight spot. He was unable to pay certain sums that he owed. The news spread like wildfire in the neighborhood, and his clients got panicky and turned against him . . . To my colleague Mourine, it's a common affair . . . There were about thirty plaintiffs in all . . . An examination of the books and papers that were seized at Villeneuve-Saint-Georges revealed, as he expected, that the bookkeeping was falsified . . . I wanted to know whether Father was one of those who filed a complaint. It seems he wasn't . . . Mourine has entrusted me, as a friend, with this memorandum book, which was seized with the rest of the documents. It's a personal favor."

He took from his pocket a black, rather large memorandum book covered with oilcloth. There was a rubber band around it.

"Jason wrote down the names and addresses of his clients and crossed out, in red ink, the names of those who died, because he worked mainly with old people . . . Father's name is in the book. Here's the page . . . As you can see, under the name and address there are only dates, without any other statement . . . It starts in September 1947 . . ."

"When Father signed our partnership agreement."

"After that he wrote down other dates, in a column: March 1948, February 1949, March 1950, and so on. Occasionally, though rarely, there's a mention of other times of the year, August, November, and once December."

Antoine handed the book back to his brother.

"I'm afraid," sighed Ferdinand, "that we're in for some unpleasant surprises. The thing that reassures me is that Father wasn't one of the plaintiffs . . . It's time for me to be going . . . I still have to let Bernard know about our appointment. Two o'clock in the office of the conciliating magistrate of the first district, on Rue du Louvre."

"I'll go down with you."

Antoine did not offer him his hand, nor did he go to see Fernande. He went straight to the kitchen and then took up his post in the second room to receive and place the customers who were beginning to arrive.

He had pasted a notice on the glass door: *The restaurant will be closed on Tuesday.*

The odor of the flowers had spread to the ground floor, where it mingled with the smells from the kitchen. He made the same gestures he made every day, uttered the same words, but he did so mechanically. Liselotte was attending to both the cloakroom and the cashier's desk.

He had not had lunch. He contented himself with eating a cold chicken leg during one of his visits to the kitchen.

François, the redheaded waiter, had taken up lunch for Fernande and the old woman. The first room was flooded with sunlight, which was reflected by the tin bar and the bottles. That morning the sun had also bathed the vegetables, fruits, and flowers in the Market, but Antoine had not particularly noticed it.

Usually, the first thing he did when he left the house in the morning was to look at the sky. Like a peasant, he could almost tell what time it was from the position of the sun, from the angle of the rays in the restaurant or the apartment.

But he had been insensitive to it since Saturday, and, the day before, he had hardly realized that spring had suddenly arrived.

When he went upstairs, his mother was in bed and Fernande was tidying up the room. A glance at her husband was enough for her to see that he was out of sorts.

"Are you upset? Is anything wrong? Was it Ferdinand's visit?"

"Not only that," he replied, waving his hand as if he were shooing off something impalpable.

"Are you going out?"

"I'm going with them to the magistrate's office. And from there we'll all go to the bank."

When he got to Rue du Louvre, he found Ferdinand waiting in the street.

"Bernard hasn't arrived yet," said his brother, looking at his watch. "He's late."

At that very moment, a car stopped at the curb. Nicole was at the wheel. Bernard seemed to be all right, though he had a faraway look in his eyes, as if he were elsewhere.

"Hello!" he called out.

And Nicole said very quickly to Ferdinand, "Don't worry. I have no intention of going with you. I wanted to be sure he'd keep his appointment. He didn't feel well this morning, and I had to give him an injection."

The magistrate handled the matter with great dispatch.

"Antoine Mature? . . . Please sign here . . . And then here . . . Thank you . . . I suppose that you are Bernard Mature and that you've been informed . . ."

"Where do I sign?"

"Here . . . And here again."

Less than ten minutes after entering the office, they received permission to open the box. Nicole and the car were no longer there.

The three brothers started walking to Boulevard de Sébastopol. They had nothing to say to each other. Each was preoccupied with his own thoughts. They walked along the streets where they had played as children, and Antoine remembered in particular the way they had played when the street cleaners, who were armed with water hoses as powerful as those of firemen, washed away the odds and ends of vegetables and other refuse. The great sport, in the summer, was to run through the jet. Ferdinand had done it too, and then Bernard. Did his brothers remember?

The manager of the Comptoir d'Escompte, a lean, dapper-looking man with grayish hair, was waiting for them. He shook hands with them when they arrived.

"This way, gentlemen."

He led them to the basement, where a uniformed guard opened a grille and then a huge iron-clad door.

"Do you have the permit from the magistrate?"

Ferdinand handed it to him.

"Fine. Who has the key?"

"Here it is."

It was embarrassing for Ferdinand to open the envelope with the five seals. The manager raised his eyebrows when he saw it.

The manager opened a first lock with a key of his own and then a second with the one that had just been given to him.

There was a moment of almost agonizing silence. The three brothers were watching as if they were in suspense, as if they half expected to find the box empty.

"If you need me, please send for me. I'm entirely at your disposal."

He walked away briskly. His new shoes squeaked. Behind the brothers were tables and chairs. In a corner, near

the grille, the impassive guard pretended to be looking elsewhere.

Ferdinand looked as if he were asking his brothers what
he should do. Then he reached into the box, took out a pile
of documents, and laid them on the table. They were stocks
and bonds, and the text of most of them was in English. They
were arranged in packets, each of which was held together
by a rubber band.

Neither of the brothers knew English. Some of the texts
were in Spanish, but the brothers did not know Spanish
either.

"We'll have to send for him," suggested Bernard.

"Unless one of you two knows what they're about."

"Would you like me to inform the manager?" asked the
guard.

"Please."

They were underground, surrounded by thick cement
that deadened all sounds. At a nearby table a woman of
about forty, who was slowly clipping coupons from a pile
of documents in front of her, occasionally glanced quizzically
at the three brothers.

What was one to make of them? They hardly dared look
at each other. The fluorescent lights made them look paler
than they were, almost greenish. They sat there as if they
were suspended in time, in space, with their eyes fixed on
the grille, the stairway, waiting for the little man who was
going to deliver his verdict.

"Did you send for me, gentlemen?"

As the two others remained silent, Ferdinand again spoke
up.

"We'd like to know the approximate value of these stocks."

The manager glanced at the first packet.

"Canadian gold mines . . ."

Then at the second.

"Colombian mines . . ."

A third, a fourth. When he came to the last packet, he looked at them in surprise.

"I suppose it was your father who bought these stocks. May I ask you whether you expect them to be worth a large sum?"

"Our father had close to a hundred thousand francs to invest every year."

"Do you know who advised him?"

"Probably a business counselor in the neighborhood."

Bernard, whose patience was exhausted, was biting his nails, as when he was a child.

"Can you take action against him?"

"He died in prison."

"That doesn't surprise me . . . I regret very much to inform you, gentlemen, that you won't get ten thousand francs for all these stocks, provided you find a buyer, which I doubt you will."

There remained in the vault a bulky manila envelope with a rubber band around it. Ferdinand's fingers trembled as he opened it.

The envelope contained four packets of bills adding up to ten thousand francs each and two thousand eight hundred and fifty francs in small bills.

The two others seemed puzzled, but Antoine had already recognized the envelope he had given his father.

"It's Papa's share of last year's profits," he explained. "I paid him that sum on February third, the day after the inventory."

"Do you still need me, gentlemen?"

Bernard broke in.

"Is there any chance of these stocks going up?"

"They're not even quoted any more. Some of them never were. As for the South American stocks, they have to do with mines that were nationalized without compensation."

"What are we to do with them?"

"Whatever you like . . . Do you want to keep the box?"

The end of the conversation was pitiful. Antoine's two brothers looked to him like ghosts that were tossing about in an unreal universe.

The trim little man took on the bearing of a kind of god who had just issued his verdict, and they almost expected to see him snicker.

What memory would he retain of his meeting with the Mature brothers?

"Where are you going?" called Ferdinand to Antoine, who had started to leave.

"Home."

"One moment . . . We'd better leave together."

He turned to the manager.

"May we keep the vault a few days?"

"In what name?"

"In the names of the three of us."

"All you need do is give a specimen signature at the desk . . . I'll prepare the forms."

Ferdinand put the stocks back into the vault. He was unable to carry them under his arm because he had no paper in which to wrap them.

"What am I to do with the money?"

"Let's go somewhere else and talk about it."

"Shall I take it?"

"I ask that we take it," said Bernard, who looked as though he were about to cry.

When they got upstairs, each of them signed a form without seeing the manager again. Outside, the sun was shining brightly. A department store was having a sale, and women were fingering linens that were being displayed on stands which were set up on the sidewalk.

"What about having a drink somewhere?"

Antoine preferred not to go back to the restaurant with them. They entered the cool shade of a big café and walked to a corner where there was hardly anyone.

Bernard ordered a cognac and his two brothers a glass of beer.

"I wonder whether Father went mad?"

"It was Jason . . ." began Ferdinand.

He broke off, waiting for the drinks to be served. Bernard gulped down his cognac and ordered another.

"Be careful. Don't forget that tomorrow's the funeral."

"I don't give a damn about the funeral."

He checked his sobs.

"You two aren't short of money . . . but if I don't shell out ten thousand francs before the end of the week, God knows where I'll be . . . Maybe in your office!" he snapped bitterly at Ferdinand. "And all because our father thought he was smarter than other people, whereas he was just an old idiot."

"It was Jason . . ."

"What do you mean, Jason?"

"We talked about it yesterday. Father trusted him."

"And Jason sold him those stocks?"

"Probably . . . Father imagined that in that way he'd

be leaving us a fantastic fortune . . . That's one of the reasons why he never talked to us about money. He wanted to surprise us."

"Why didn't he lodge a complaint when Jason was arrested?"

Antoine, who was lost in a kind of reverie, was asking himself the same question. He barely heard what his brothers were saying. He was the one who had known their father best, and he imagined how terrible a blow it must have been to the old man when he learned that the man he had trusted was nothing but a swindler.

To have lodged a complaint along with the others would have been to admit he had been naïve. It would also have been to admit to his sons that he was not leaving them the inheritance they were expecting.

He had worked all his life, ever since the age of twelve, to accumulate a fortune, counting every penny, and all that remained of it was the restaurant, which was really run by Antoine.

He had lived for months with a sense of shame, knowing that when he was gone he would leave behind him bitterness instead of regret.

Antoine had the feeling that he had never understood his father so well, his peasant character, his humbleness and pride.

"What do we do with the money?" asked Bernard at last. He was so impatient and so filled with anguish that he could no longer bear it.

For him it was exactly as when he went to see one of his brothers about a loan. He would start by asking for thousands of francs for a terrific deal. Little by little he would reach the point of being satisfied with two or three hundred francs, mere pocket money.

He had just lost a fortune. The future had collapsed in a few minutes. There nevertheless were bank notes in Ferdinand's pocket, bills that he could feel, that would enable him to deal with what was most urgent, to delude himself for a few weeks, to feel that he was on the crest of a wave.

"What do you think, Antoine?"

"You can divide it between you, as partial payment of what I owe you for the restaurant."

"Don't you want us to sign a receipt?"

"I don't need a receipt."

He stood up.

"If you don't mind, Fernande's waiting for me."

He had no desire to be present when the money was divided amidst the glasses on the table, beneath the eyes of the indifferent waiter.

VIII

One would have thought that the whole little world of the Market, all the storekeepers in the neighborhood, were meeting on Rue de la Grande-Truanderie. Old Chaussard, dressed up in his Sunday best, was standing very erect on the sidewalk opposite the restaurant. Beside him was his son, who was wearing a black suit and black tie.

Women had come as they were, in their old work clothes, abandoning their stalls for a moment, and there were some who were drying their eyes with the corner of an apron.

Gabriel, the second cousin from Riom, had brought his wife and three children, and they were standing in the mortuary chapel, where there was no longer room enough for those who walked by the coffin at the last minute.

Fernande, Véronique, and Nicole remained behind, while the three brothers walked side by side behind the hearse, which was moving slowly in the direction of the Church of Saint-Eustache.

The air was mild. The sun was shining again. Behind the brothers, the dark crowd wound its way over three hundred yards, and the bells were tolling in a cloudless sky.

The brothers did not say a word. Nor did they look at each other. The master of ceremonies, who was wearing a two-pointed hat, led them to their places in the first row, in the semidarkness of the church, and they remained standing while the chairs grated behind them on the stone floor.

The rear door remained open, for the crowd overflowed into the street. A big diamond-shaped patch of sunlight stood out in the dimness.

At the offertory, everyone put his hand into his pocket mechanically.

"*Pater Noster . . .*"

The priest, who was wearing a black chasuble, walked around the catafalque and swung the censer. A young choirboy trotted behind him and knelt in front of the tabernacle as he went by.

"*Et ne nos inducas in tentationem . . .*"

The voices of the choirboys in the rood-loft flooded every nook and corner of the huge nave.

"Amen . . ."

Antoine's face was flushed, and he could feel that his ears were red. The following day, he would find all the men and women who filled the church back at their posts in the Market and around it, as if nothing had happened. Around 7 A.M., after talking with Léon behind the red iron bars of the butcher shop, he would ask Jules to give him his morning cup of coffee. In a few years the Market would disappear. The sheds would be dismantled as if they were children's toys. The façades of the houses would come down first, then the floors and stairways, revealing wallpaper with marks of furniture.

The man in the two-pointed hat touched Antoine's sleeve. Antoine followed him. Or rather he followed Ferdinand, who, as eldest brother, led the procession.

Outside, people were jostling each other. Not only was the hearse loaded with flowers, but two cars were needed to transport all the other wreaths and bouquets.

All one could see was heads, hundreds of heads, and,

somewhere above them, the stiff banner of the Auvergnats of Paris.

As Antoine went by, someone—he didn't know who—shook his hand furtively. A moment later he was in one of the cars with his brothers.

It took another ten minutes for the funeral procession to get under way. In the car in front of them Antoine could see the priest's white surplice and the blond hair of the choirboy.

They drove slowly through the Market between two hedges of silent spectators. When they reached the quais of the Seine, the cars began to speed up.

The three brothers sat quietly, without speaking, as if each were ignoring the others' presence. They were now riding between rows of houses. There were balconies, with clothes drying on the railings. Then they came to the suburbs, with their low-cost housing projects and empty lots.

Cars passed them. The passengers turned around to see the hearse and tried to make out the faces of the people in the cars that were following it.

Flowers were budding, and little tufts of delicate green grass were sprouting. Trees were flowering here and there. Powerful jets were watering the land around the walls of a truck garden, and a woman was bending over and picking leeks.

In a little while they would be back in the restaurant, in the Sideshow, where tables had been set up side by side, as for a wedding.

They would again see Gabriel, the stationmaster, and his wife, and the old woman who lived in Saint-Hippolyte and of whom they had caught only a glimpse, and others too who were more or less related to the family, people who for a brief spell had played a part in their father's life.

Was it really Auguste who was in the hearse which they saw from time to time when it rounded a corner?

To Antoine, perhaps to others too, he was not only dead. He no longer existed. Nothing of him remained. Nor had he left anything behind.

There had once been the sixteen-year-old blonde girl with tousled hair whose photograph he had kept in his wallet all his life. There had been the restaurant in the Market, with its sausages and hams and huge loaves of bread, the restaurant in the photograph which he had been proudly showing to a couple a moment before being struck down and dragging the tablecloth and dishes along with him.

There had been children, first Ferdinand, then Antoine, then Bernard, all of whom had crawled at one time or another in the sawdust.

They had been a family. Auguste had had a wife and three sons.

A wife who now had to be spoon-fed and whose signature had been stolen the night before so that it could be transformed into money as fast as possible.

Three sons who had been brothers, who had slept together, who had all been afraid of the dark, who had all known the same joy of romping in the sun.

All three of them were now sitting in the car, all of them silent, without anything to say to each other, without daring to speak, because old Auguste was dead and they had become strangers.

All that remained in the Market was the tin bar and the hams and sausages in the window. When the house itself disappeared, Antoine and Fernande would probably build a hotel somewhere, preferably by the sea, and they would grow old together without leaving anything behind, except money that would be squabbled over by Jean-Loup's children, perhaps by those of Marie-Laure too if ever she married, and by Bernard grown old and still in quest of a fortune.

Antoine looked at the two faces in front of him.

They were as empty as his.

Épalinges
March 17, 1966